THE INNER HARBOUR

ALSO BY ANTOINE VOLODINE
PUBLISHED BY THE UNIVERSITY OF MINNESOTA PRESS

SOLO VIOLA

MEVLIDO'S DREAMS

THE
INNER
HARBOUR

ANTOINE VOLODINE

TRANSLATED BY GINA M. STAMM

A UNIVOCAL BOOK

UNIVERSITY OF MINNESOTA PRESS

Minneapolis

London

Originally published in French as *Le port intérieur*, copyright 1996/2010 by Les Éditions de Minuit

Translation copyright 2025 by the Regents of the University of Minnesota

All rights reserved. No part of this publication may be reproduced, stored in a retrieval system, utilized for purposes of training artificial intelligence technologies, or transmitted in any form or by any means, electronic, mechanical, photocopying, recording, or otherwise, without the prior written permission of the publisher.

Published by the University of Minnesota Press
111 Third Avenue South, Suite 290
Minneapolis, MN 55401-2520
http://www.upress.umn.edu

ISBN 978-1-5179-1969-6 (pb)

A Cataloging-in-Publication record for this book is available from the Library of Congress.

Printed in the United States of America on acid-free paper

The University of Minnesota is an equal-opportunity educator and employer.

34 33 32 31 30 29 28 27 26 25   10 9 8 7 6 5 4 3 2 1

CONTENTS

Translator's Note — vii
Dialogue — 1
Fiction — 9
Logbook — 21
Dream — 30
Fiction — 43
Monologue — 48
Logbook — 54
Fiction — 61
Monologue — 76
Fiction — 83
Fiction — 92
Dream — 101
Monologue — 117
Fiction — 122
Monologue — 139

TRANSLATOR'S NOTE

Formerly, I, Zhuang Zhou, dreamt that I was a butterfly, a butterfly flying about, feeling that it was enjoying itself. I did not know that it was Zhou. Suddenly I awoke, and was myself again, the veritable Zhou. I did not know whether it had formerly been Zhou dreaming that he was a butterfly, or it was now a butterfly dreaming that it was Zhou.
—Zhuang Zhou, *The Writings of Kwang-Sze*, Trans. James Legge (1891)

This well-known paradox from classical Taoism appears in photonegative in Antoine Volodine's prose, where neither we nor the protagonist Breughel fully know what is reality and what is a dream. But in this case, we have to choose between nightmares. Is Breughel a washed-up novelist on the lam whose glamorous lover Gloria went mad and died tragically, leaving him in a sort of half-life in the slums of Macau? Or is he a hero in one of his own novels, bravely putting his life on the line to keep a killer from finding what is left of Gloria in a mental institution? Or is the dream not even Breughel's, but the "dark war" in Gloria's mind where an army kills a frightened elephant in a crowd of refugees, and then sells out a transport ship (whose passengers include Breughel) to menacing "chrysalids the size of orcas"?

In *The Inner Harbour*, the reader slips from one reality to another, all of them flowing from Breughel's mouth or pen. Is he in control of the narrative, or merely one of its victims and its scribe? The fragments of his writing vacillate between past and present, from a first-person narrator to an outside observer's standpoint. The sentences in stream of consciousness, woven from the minds of the interrogator and the man being questioned, can be vertiginous, breaking off as a train of thought is dropped and picked up somewhere else entirely. And as always with the post-exotic, the language itself exists in an uncanny valley where it is and is not quite our own, what Volodine has called "a foreign literature in French."

At the same time, there is much that is familiar for the reader aware of trends in the novels of the twilight of France's own colonial empire, in particular the *nouveau roman* in both form and content. The intense descriptions of place in *The Inner Harbour* call to mind the India and Indochina cycles of Marguerite Duras, as do the dialogues representing interrogation and psychological instability. The investigatory structure also evokes the way in which Alain Robbe-Grillet claimed that the detective novel could exemplify the future of the French novel by providing a situation in which characters can resist the various interpretations the author or reader attempts to impose on them. Thus *The Inner Harbour* is inscribed within a tradition of literary experimentation, all the while pushing the boundaries of that tradition and painting an vivid tableau of a late-colonial Asian city.

THE INNER HARBOUR

DIALOGUE

Your mouth is trembling. You would like to not talk anymore. You would like to go back to the darkness and not to have to describe the darkness. The best thing would be to lie down in the amnesia, at the edges of reality, eyes half-closed, and to stay like that until your last breath, mummified beneath a murky film of murky consciousness and silence.

But, sadly, you don't manage to stay silent.

A man is there, very close by, attentive to what is emerging. He is threatening, he is listening. He threatens again, he listens. You try to avoid his gaze. Nevertheless, if your lips are trembling, it isn't out of fear of pain or death. It is instead the old urge to chatter that moves them. You believed for too long that talking would weave something useful on top of reality, in which you could wrap yourself up and hide, something protective. Talking or writing. You were wrong. Words, like everything else, destroy.

Let's get to the point, said Kotter.

What, said Breughel.

Stop mumbling, said Kotter. Tell me what you have to say. Let's get this over with.

Yes, said Breughel.

Start with Machado, the Brazilian, suggested Kotter.

He's dead, said Breughel.

You have to start with someone; why not with him, said Kotter.

He was sick, said Breughel. He died much too soon. He left us in Chinese territory, Gloria and me, exiled on the banks of the Pearl River, in a holding pattern. After that, we just survived. Nothing happened that I had prepared myself for, neither the worry nor the happiness. Then time became motionless.

Ideal for growing old painlessly, said Kotter.

What? I said.

Nothing, said Kotter. Keep going, Breughel. The Pearl River.

The Pearl River, I sighed. A superb delta. Canton, Macau, Zhuhai, Hong Kong.

I know, said Kotter. I flew over it on my way here. Superb, yes. Magnificent. Try as you might to find the words to describe it, to paint it, you can't.

Yes, I said. That color of the sea near the coast. A shade of green unknown in the West.

Two or three empty seconds passed. The poorly ventilated room dripped with humidity. Most of the objects exuded disagreeable smells. The sink, the books, the dirty or half-dirty clothes, the bed. Kotter raised his hand again. On his left fist sweat was gleaming.

So, Machado, Breughel began again. A friend. And I say friend to pay homage to him and because it's what I think. We kept him in our hearts, Gloria and I. Without his help, we would never have had a chance to make it out alive. Paradise would have caught up with us within three weeks.

What Paradise, asked Kotter.

You, said Breughel. The ones who sent you.

Ah, said Kotter. That's how you.

Yes, said Breughel. The name was invented by Machado. We never spoke of you openly, even in whispers. As you well know, there is always an unkind ear lurking behind the walls. A hostile intelligence.

Exactly, said Kotter. You have to talk in code.

We also used to say the Party, continued Breughel. After all, we were a kind of dissident cell. That gave a fake political dimension to our story. Leftist chords vibrated around us like a halo.

A dissident cell, angels, muttered Kotter.

Oh, minor angels, said Breughel. Who feared being executed by razor blade or lead before being able to enjoy what.

Come on, said Kotter, the way you carry on, Breughel.

Before being able to enjoy love, for example, or illusions of liberty and.

Calm down, intervened Kotter. Continue with Machado. His role in your exile.

Gloria and I, we had the intention of disappearing into nature. But it's very complicated when you have killers hot on your heels. Very risky.

Killers, you're exaggerating, said Kotter.

Aah, said Breughel. And you. But I had thought that you.

Enough, said Kotter. We were on Machado. I'm listening.

The operation would have failed, said Breughel. Disappearing with no blunders. I would have scuttled everything with my naïve little amateur ruses. He, Machado, wasn't like that, he had worked undercover during the urban guerilla warfare. He was someone who could get along perfectly in parallel worlds. Twenty-four hours was enough for him to get a complete set of falsified passports. And the forger didn't cheat him, didn't cut his throat after the money was handed over. He was a master of evasive techniques. Gloria could also have acted. She had training as. She had been educated with Machado, in the same circumstances.

Not exactly with him, nor at the same time, ventured Kotter.

I don't know anything about it. Doesn't matter. She never talked about Paradise from before my arrival, almost never. She kept quiet about her responsibilities within the machinery. What I mean is, she could have taken care of the problem. But psychological disturbances kept her from being effective. I didn't realize at the time, I had just met her. Machado understood the disaster we were running toward, and, out of sympathy, he decided to take the plunge with us.

Disturbances.

Yes. The Party had noticed, no? A mental fracture that was growing in her and that. Beneath a film of dreadful visions her personality was secretly changing shape. It had already smothered her perception of the world. All acuity in her gaze. She would lose patience over nothing, she had begun to reason obliquely and tortuously, explaining the inexplicable endlessly, with arguments she got from dreams. Being around her day after day, you saw that she wasn't assessing the impacts of her actions well. Don't tell me, Kotter, that the Party was unaware.

You seem to have been pretty unaware yourself.

Paradise was compartmentalized. The Party. I had never heard of Gloria before I met her. I had no reason to start digging into her past with a critical eye. I don't have a calling for psychiatric enquiries. We immediately fell into each other's arms. Passion, Kotter, I don't think you can totally understand it. Described everywhere, in millions of books, but never lived after all. A very beautiful, luminous passion. We immediately planned to flee. To forget Paradise forever. I didn't have any idea that. She, on the other hand, knew everything about me, because her mission was to seduce me. There is, so it seems, a full dossier on each target. Gloria had studied mine.

Breughel seemed to pause. Kotter insisted. Physically he insisted, without saying anything.

Machado also knew me by heart, Breughel began again. He dived with us through the looking glass. He guided all our movements. We were vulnerable, within firing range, and suddenly, in the space of one morning, Machado had drawn around us an opaque screen. Everything had to be obfuscated in a very short time, he explained. We had to reduce the ties binding us to a thread, then jump out of the entanglement. Then cut ourselves off, giving one last knife blow. Then we could begin to live again. At least if, he concluded, we had stocks of gold and courage.

Breughel sighed.

Courage. We were senseless enough to have more than we needed, all three of us. As for our financial situation, it wasn't a. Gloria was rich.

With money stolen from the Party, said Kotter.

Oh no, said Breughel.

Stolen money, insisted Kotter.

Oh, said Breughel, we didn't rob anyone. We don't steal from little old ladies. Gloria had access to anonymous accounts. She took advantage of it. If you call that theft.

She embezzled a fortune, said Kotter.

Oh, a fortune. A large amount. And of that.

And of that what, asked Kotter.

Of that, Machado only withdrew an insignificant percentage for himself, just enough to buy himself the medicine and drugs that calmed him when the pain came on, more and more often and more and more intensely. Pocket money before exiting the stage, he said. He knew he was condemned to death before too long and he felt only indifference for dollars. Nothing interested him anymore except our escape. He cherished our success with an artist's tenderness.

The Brazilian accompanied us to a safe place in Southeast Asia, he settled us in Macau after having sown several false tracks behind us, clues that would lead the Party's investigator nowhere. In a few hours, thanks to Machado's personal channels, thanks to his Libano-Brazilian network we had acquired Portuguese citizenship. That gave us the right to stay indefinitely in Macau, with no trouble until the territory's return to the Chinese authority. I know you aren't particularly competent, Machado told me as he gave me my papers and listed the advantages and drawbacks of my new citizenship, you're even rather idiotic in your own way, but, between now and 1999, you will have the time to change. Or to make arrangements for what comes after.

You spoke Portuguese at the time? Asked Kotter.

Yes, I said. But Gloria, especially.

Normal, Kotter pointed out. She had lived with Machado for three years. Swimming in the language every day. Great for fluency and intonation.

Breughel went quiet.

His lips were trembling. His mouth, too, shook from the emotion, from the memories.

The air was sticky.

You could hear Breughel's anxious breathing and that, more martial, of Kotter. Then Paradise's assassin made an aggressive gesture. He wanted more words. Breughel acquiesced.

Yes, he said. For four months, Machado tested the system that he had set up and that guaranteed our safety. We had good reason to imagine that the Party's bloodhounds, Paradise's, were leaning toward the wrong hypotheses and that they had us located in the opposite direction from where we ended up. But be careful, warned Machado. The time that's passed can be deceiving. You'll have to be vigilant for ten years, fifty years. Until the end.

It's true, observed Kotter. Time doesn't matter.

The awful sickness was ravaging him, continued Breughel. He could feel himself on the way out, he gave me instructions for survival, to hold up when he was no longer there. Gloria's psychological state alarmed him as much as it did me. I warn you, Breughel, he would murmur. You're heading toward some painful times with her. It's possible that she'll get back on her feet, but I get the impression that things will get worse for you. You'll have to take care of her. Even if the pain becomes very painful indeed. You understand me, Breughel? Swear to me that. I swore. I was sincere. My love for Gloria was in no way a passing fancy, and besides, I had reached an age where you fatalistically accept the constraints imposed by an unsolitary life. You spend your life bowing to a sense of duty, to absurd responsibilities, but, when middle age comes, you suddenly discover the calculations hidden behind it all, the hope that you will be able to die less ignobly than the others, in a decline softened by the absence of shame. And yet, you.

Let's go back to the Brazilian, suggested Kotter.

The Brazilian's health was visibly declining, said Breughel. He started avoiding us. He dedicated his last energy to haunting Macau's saunas. He would fondle the Russian or Chinese prostitutes who plied their trade in the big hotels, at the doors of casinos or bars. I met him from time to time not far from his house, in front of the A-Ma temple, pale, skeletal. Then I didn't see him anymore. He had warned me that he would melt away with no goodbye. Then he wasn't with us anymore. He had erased all trace of his time there. In his apartment, he. In the apartment he had occupied for two or three months, some Filipinos had moved in.

Filipinos.

Yes. Every region has its subaltern peoples. Fifteen or so women were piled into living quarters meant for a couple after that.

Continue, said Kotter.

Both of us, Gloria and I, we adored that man.

Continue, repeated Kotter.

It often would happen that Gloria would call me Machado, would confuse me with Machado, at different times of day and even in the middle of the night, by mistake or cruelty. She would look at me after that with an unwholesome look, as if contemplating an unflattering comparison with me, and, me, I readied myself to hear her express her distress, an evaluation to my disadvantage, and between us arose a violent sadness, the feeling of an irreparable loss, but then we didn't speak, and nothing horrible, on this subject, was pronounced by myself or her. I looked at Gloria in silence, as inaudible whispers escaped her lips. Then she fell silent.

FICTION

At this point, the year of the Goat passed, then the year of the Monkey, then that of the Rooster. Breughel inhabited a now-indistinct span of time, but he hadn't yet broken with the idea of some measurement of duration, of the sounds we use to date, of this kind of. Here he is, as it happens, studying the Chinese names of the twelve cardinal animals of the zodiac. He had just recited them in order, having begun with *Lao Shu*, the Rat, and he was wiping away the sweat drenching his brow when he felt on his temple the end of a tube that seemed to have a caliber greater than thirty-two hundredths of an inch, and whose presence at that spot was of a rather disturbing character.

Breughel got up and moved around the room, not without recreating certain poses he had learned long ago, when he was young and active and he regularly practiced techniques of hand-to-hand combat against clubs, broken bottles, or cutlasses, but whose naturalness and reflexivity he had neglected to keep up, burying them under a decade of physical idleness and skepticism, and, after a minute ruled by confusion, he sat back down. A man who, for ease, we'll call Kotter, again pressed his weapon against Breughel's left temple. Let's say once and for all that the diameter of the barrel was about thirty-two hundredths of an inch and leave it at that.

You have something to tell us, declared Kotter.

Oh, I don't know about that, said Breughel.

He wasn't unhappy to be there, on a stable seat, recovering from the vicious blows he had received on the rib cage, and which had provoked in him a feeling of fatigue, even of torpor. He was puffing like a buffalo. He didn't react when Kotter put a rope around his neck. The cord didn't tighten around his neck, but it fixed his head to the back of the chair. Kotter must have had his reasons for doing this. You might think, for example, that he wished to prevent any further pathetic demonstrations of jiu-jitsu, without at the same time depriving Breughel of his right of speech.

Go on, said Kotter.

He was also breathing heavily. His clothing, poorly adapted to the temperature, was forming damp patches and creases. The jacket of a primary school teacher on vacation, a green shirt, jeans.

You could hear the exhalations whose violence slowly decreased.

To that were suddenly added noises from outside.

On the other side of the door, indeed, in the alley crushed beneath malodorous heat, an old woman was puttering around, with the intent of listening to a Chinese opera cassette tape. She had arranged her largest bones on a microscopic stool that held her about ten centimeters from the ground. Then she was manipulating a cheap little cassette player that was moderately resisting her, and which finally, after all, quite reasonably, bent to her will. Gongs and cymbals announced the beginning of the act. At that point she fell silent.

To himself, Breughel called her Mrs. Fong, but didn't know her name. Like Breughel's other neighbors, she was running out the time remaining to her in loneliness and indigence, and, toward this foreign devil, despite the formal courtesies he lavished upon her, she harbored a faint racist hostility. Her relationship with Breughel, for months now, was built upon a lack of eye contact and an ostentatious indifference. If the killer lost his cool and if Mrs. Fong heard a shot, screams, a moan of distress, she wouldn't modify her behavior. She would make herself believe that a private party amongst barbarians was going on with ordinary brawling and firecrackers. She would take no interest for any reason and, afterwards—if there was an after—her testimony wouldn't provide anything for the investigators.

Breughel forced himself to forget this bony pauperess in black trousers, as well as the narrow- and hard-eyed police who would take care of his corpse. With an exhausted gaze, he took in the disarray that covered the room, then he squinted as if the half-light was painful to him.

At that moment, he caught a whiff of the polyethylene of the pistol Kotter was brandishing. It would have been useless to seek out the mixture of steel and oil that fills the surroundings of a real firearm. The thing was fake. A toy, maybe. Yes. No doubt a toy that Kotter had gotten for himself, in a five-and-dime in Macau or Hong Kong.

A plastic replica, brand new.

Discovering that he was at the mercy of an innocuous 9mm irritated Breughel a little. Nonetheless, he kept his thoughts to himself and, quite the contrary, respected the ritual progression of anxiety when facing death, as he had often described it in his novels, back when he knew how to break an attacker's arms and when he still attributed importance to the publication and fate of his books. The sweat running down his sides grew cold and. He was beginning to hiccup out this last thoughts.

Inside his skull, short films sparkled, little, quick, silent movies.

The photographs came one after another, constantly overlapping. At the speed of light passed by the joys of childhood, several dogs, cats, adults, marionettes, vast and elaborate fistfights with his little brother, the resinous color of the gifts under the Christmas tree, and, immediately thereafter, because time was short, he skipped over forty years and a marriage to rejoin the most recent period of his existence, the one in which he had loved Gloria Vancouver.

Now, on that overloaded screen, appeared Gloria.

He saw her again on a Mediterranean beach, coming toward him to seduce him in accordance with the orders that she'd been given, then the day after their first night, on the same beach, she is covering herself with suncream and talking to him, then, with no transition, when they had already betrayed the Party together, Paradise, she was already with him on the other side of the world, facing the overwhelming green of Hong Kong's port, and they were both silent, and they were both overwhelmed, while Machado strafed Victoria Harbour with an Olympus camera, and he saw her later in an airport setting, maybe Manilla or Taipei, or Bangkok, and she was nonchalantly holding out her false Portuguese papers to a border guard, and later still he was in front of the final sequence where he played a supporting role, in the background, she was separated from him by about one hundred meters and he was observing her from afar, in the crowd, without running toward her, he stared at her, his mind empty, and she was lying on the asphalt of a central avenue in Seoul, as if asleep in the middle of traffic, surrounded by Koreans and blood. Surrounded by blood.

The last scene embedded itself in him with such intensity that it blotted out Kotter, the chair, the synthetic pistol. He floated between nothingness and love, disembodied, outside of time, barely perspiring.

Then a man tugged on the cord around his neck. It was a cord studded with little barbs, a kind common in Europe but extremely rare here, in the shops of Southern China. The killer must have brought it with him in his luggage. The pressure on the cartilage of his neck grew sharper, irritating, irritated, almost breaking the skin.

But Gloria.

Gloria was covering her stomach with suncream, her legs, and she was talking to him. The memory had no sound, none of the conversation came back. You had to be satisfied with the landscape, the circumstances. Maybe, as they often did in those first days, they were telling each other about their dreams. Gloria excelled at making up stories on that subject. He was sitting next to her on the pebble beach.

I was sitting next to you on the stones. I was thinking about the intoxication of the previous night, about our vertigo, and I hesitated to conclude from that that we had signed some sort of lasting alliance. Declarations had been babbled out, but you never know for sure, at the beginning, if that feverishness is a theatrical demonstration or a door opening onto unwritten legends. You had been sincere, you revealed the Party's intentions to me—you didn't call it the Party or Paradise but the Islands, as if it were a coastline of exotic hopes we would always be nostalgic for, you had described the manipulation of which I was supposed to be, with you as an intermediary, the willing victim, but I didn't yet know how far I could trust you. I didn't know if you had faked lovemaking magnificently, I didn't know if you had really abandoned all the lies. Your youth made me vulnerable. I didn't feel worthy of you and I was anxious being near you, fearing humiliation, the peal of laughter that would shatter my illusions and would leave me ridiculous facing the waves, with the twenty years I have on you, the disgust, the shame. I feared the worst. We had a lot to learn about one another.

Breughel took off his sunglasses. The crests of the waves took on a mauve hue, the sky was blazing. He had never had a mistress as dangerous, as beautiful, as strange, as mysterious, as subtle, and as.

I'm listening, Kotter began again. Machado, Gloria Vancouver, the money. You know what brings me here.

The people you're talking about are dead, said Breughel. The money has gone up in smoke. Kill me, Kotter. You don't have anything to worry about, the neighbor won't tell anyone. Fire. I'm ready.

Come on, come on, scolded Kotter. No childishness.

He looked for a handkerchief in his military jacket. None of his numerous pockets contained one.

Outside, the opera cassette played on, with distortions and sobs.

The shrill voices of Chinese actresses can verge on the sublime, but Kotter's non-Asian eardrums were not yet capable of understanding. The voice wound about above the puddles and trash dotting Tarrafeiro Alley, the little passage where Breughel now was staying. It came to curl around the killer and inspired a grimace from him, then unwound itself around Breughel. The latter man recalled many stage shows. In the space of a second he relived long, very long performances in front of temples, under bamboo awnings, in the stuffiness exacerbated by mosquitos, beneath giant ceiling fans, at night.

I didn't understand anything that was happening onstage. Generals with painted faces arguing with dazzling princesses, getting betrothed, marrying, plotting in parade uniforms, their heads topped with endlessly tall feathers, magnificent, their backs studded with flags. I heard you. You were whispering commentaries in my ear. Because you were there up against me, as close as can be. Mentally inaccessible but physically close. I was seeking your body. I put my hand on your arm. We were covered in sweat. You were inventing a hallucinated storyline whose themes resembled those that tortured you in your dreams. The dark war, the deserters, the voyage to the islands, the chrysalids. I was trying to follow along, and I was agreeing, even if there was nothing in common between your madness and the subject of the opera. With emotion, I took in what you were telling me. I could feel that, later on, I would write this down, when I was alone, so that I could believe in our reconciliation, so that I could believe that you.

There was carefreeness in the air. The public was chatting, eating, coming and going. The noise of traffic added to the hubbub of the audience. Sometimes the ambient noise grew to the point that only the gongs and cymbals had enough strength to pierce through. At the beginning of each act, a magic lantern was activated to project the lyrics sung by the singers onto a vertical banner. Then the machinery would jam, and the prop master would suddenly have a fit of rage and turn it off. You would tell me which characters you had recognized and picked up as they flew by. You were making progress in Chinese, I wasn't.

Gather your thoughts, Breughel, said Kotter. We're not going to stay here like this without saying anything.

The barrel of the gun pressed against Breughel's temple. The cord was cutting into his neck beneath his Adam's apple.

I want you to tell me where Gloria Vancouver is hiding, demanded Kotter.

My memory doesn't work anymore, complained Breughel. It's Macau, the heat, the humidity. The deprivation of silence. I forget everything.

His panting was becoming hoarse, and suddenly a tragic tone crept in, a sincerity that wasn't mere querulousness.

Kotter wasn't insensitive. He loosened the cord.

You can't imagine what. Living constantly in this waterlogged atmosphere, said Breughel. In this noise. All hours of day and night, your intelligence takes on water, is diluted by the steam and the din. The echoes of the din. You can never rest, Kotter. You have no idea of.

His fifty-year-old-man's eyelids fluttered. They stayed closed. He was worn out and damp.

Kotter moved his gun one centimeter to avoid a drop of sweat. He had seen it well up at the gray hairline and now it was rolling down.

I wrote, began Breughel.

What, said Kotter. What did you.

I was waiting for you, said Breughel. Someone like you was always going to come eventually, sent by Paradise, with a pistol to my head. Someone I named Kotter. Dimitri or John Kotter, depending on how I felt. That name doesn't bother you, does it.

It's all the same to me, said Kotter.

I put together some notes for Kotter to consult after assassinating me. Because I guess that.

What kind of notes, demanded Kotter.

Remarks on Macau, various fictions, portraits of Gloria, dream stories, listed off Breughel. Various novelistic moments. Gloria's or my dreams.

Doesn't interest me.

He had changed his firing angle. If, extraordinarily, a bullet were to burst forth, it would traverse the darkness of the brain and come out his right eye. Then it would end its trajectory in the wall.

Don't feel like reading, said Kotter. No time.

Breughel murmured his regrets.

Too bad, he said. I wrote all of that for.

Kotter, abruptly, lost patience.

And the money? could be heard, while a sharp traction pulled on the cord, once again causing Breughel respiratory difficulty. You spent it all?

The choking went on. There were spasms. The spectacle had nothing in it worth describing. There you had only ugliness and raw survival.

What money said Breughel, as soon as this period of censorship ended.

Now he inserted his hand between the cartilage of his trachea and the cord. Kotter made him let go.

And Gloria Vancouver, said Kotter. I don't see any trace of her in this dump.

He gestured toward the bedroom with his head.

She dumped you? He said.

Breughel was massaging his neck and the spots on his body where the pain, after having flared up, was stagnating. Kotter had twisted his arm, and as he had continued to fight back, he had pistol-whipped the back of his head. The pistol had metallic parts, but, above all, Kotter knew how to hit. You learn that in Paradise's schools in the special sections. The points where the nerves are close to the surface. The fragile spots.

If you don't cooperate, said Kotter, I'm going to put a bullet in your kneecap.

Breughel shrugged his shoulders.

He seemed very exhausted, but in reality he wasn't cracking. We were far from that mental meltdown that sometimes, in enhanced interrogations, sets off an uninterrupted flood of confessions, a torrent of self-criticism and unvarnished truth. We were far from that.

You heard? Demanded Kotter.

Breughel didn't move. He had laid his hands on his thighs. You might have thought he was dozing off.

This heat, wheezed Kotter. Couldn't we turn on a fan?

He pointed with his index finger at a piece of junk.

Good god, exhaled Kotter again. And this mess.

On the table sat a typewriter and a tray with a teapot and bowl. Papers were all over. Some pages were covered with Chinese characters and others not. Crates from a grocery store were being used to store sheaves of paper, clothes, books, food. On the concrete floor, under the bed, newspapers and notebooks were stacked up. There were motionless cockroaches between the piles, who must have eaten the poison of the omnipresent anti-roach sweets. Everything gave off the scent of degrading cellulose, of old damp cloth. Everything was sticky.

The handwritten and typed sheets lay in the sparse light, in this atmosphere like that of a paupers' sauna, and, softened by the musty air, they seemed to be waiting mournfully for a man to want to choose one or another of them and to pick it up and peruse it, to explore it in every direction with ferocity, then to return it to the shadows.

Machado must have left you too, guessed Kotter. He wasn't a guy who would have tolerated this pigsty. He left you, didn't he?

Breughel didn't answer.

Time passed fruitlessly.

Kotter shrugged his shoulders in turn.

Even though the plastic pistol continued to point at one of Breughel's kneecaps—the right one—the action wasn't progressing.

On the other side of the door, the two-stringed violin and the moon-shaped mandolin paused. *Jing hu*, *er hu* and *yue qin* are the names of these instruments, but who cares? Regardless, the orchestra marked a pause. Unaccompanied by the musicians, the soprano discoursed in a mode halfway between singing and recitation, in groups of four or five syllables.

I loved this kind of passage. That day, as usual, I couldn't manage to pick out the smallest translatable phoneme. The melancholic arc of Cantonese flitted through the silence of the alley. It invaded the torrid hour, the recesses and the trash bins, the pile of stinking scrap metal, and the boards that no one thought to get rid of. The vowels rang out with extreme clarity, brightly colored, endlessly bounding from height to height. Each half-phrase was punctuated by a clash of cymbals.

Breughel listened. He no longer opened his mouth.

Seeing Kotter's bad-tempered expression, you knew that the killer wasn't satisfied with the direction the interview was taking. The exchange between the two interlocutors seemed to have run dry. Each one was sweating in his own corner. Nothing decisive happened.

Now, Kotter was stretching his legs. He tripped in a plate full of granules for the rats or cockroaches, then he avoided an overturned chair, some t-shirts.

Sweat darkened the sides of his jacket. Drops ran down his cheeks. He headed toward the pale green mass of the refrigerator. The motivation of this movement was, apparently, the fan he had alluded to shortly before. Soon he was there. He flipped the switch. The button toggled with a crisp, promising sound. But neither the motor nor the blades budged.

Doesn't work, piece of trash, he said.

The soprano had made her way across her melodious solo, she had made it to the other side, and, once more, the orchestra accompanied her, in unison, once more it went along with her, overlooking no happy reunion. From this point on a flute participated in the adventure. Its name in Mandarin is *di zi*, but Kotter obviously didn't feel like.

It doesn't work, does it? he asked Brueghel.

I should have been able to identify the opera or the excerpt of the opera that Mrs. Fong and I were enjoying, separated by a rusty door and two thousand years of immiscible traditions, her squatting on her tiny stool in the middle of the trash cluttering Tarrafeiro Alley, and me on my chair, surrounded by useless deaths and memories. I should have been able to name this piece. That's how you do things in literature.

But the pressure of the pistol on my temple had created turbulence in my memory, and I hesitated between *Mu Gui Ying Accepts the Seal of Command* and *The Magnolia Flower*, not ruling out, as a third hypothesis, *The Treason of Wong Fui*.

I stayed like that for several minutes, dubious and speechless, exuding brine from every pore.

Kotter refreshed his face under the tap of the kitchen sink.

Regarding everything else, when you think about the only thing that matters for me, dreams of Gloria, everything else is only unimportant accidents, small details.

LOGBOOK

I

Your memory isn't working. It's not managing to.

And yet it's not for lack of trying. Lost hours, thousands of them. The Chinese words are there, just too far away, not too timid, but as soon as you've caught one, it escapes. You just need to. A blink of your consciousness, half an hour of torpor, and already the fugitive has rejoined the noisy street, the mass where every character is unknown, to learn or relearn.

You're there, in front of this oceanic language, on the edge of the Chinese world, on a precarious little beachhead where you collect the elementary, mismatched expressions thanks to which you would really like to avoid being taken for an aphasic barbarian, but nothing comes to your tongue or to your mind.

So you say nothing.

And three years go by like this, in this city that was once a pirate haven, and that now is content to be a seedy annex of the People's Republic, neither more nor less gangrened, moreover, neither more nor less odious than the other global hubs where the underworld of billionaire capitalism writhes.

Three years and a bit.

Breughel no longer writes or he writes very little, a few texts without poetry, which he doesn't correct. The old lights are extinguished. What he is exploring doesn't. He agonizes on the berm of the imaginary. He no longer travels anywhere except within physical, intellectual decline. What he is exploring is not being reborn in the form of a book.

He doesn't remember his dreams very well.

He hasn't communicated with anyone, since Gloria Vancouver and Machado died.

Nothing happens. He moves forward, he wanders in the stifling heat, beneath the unexpressed but general disdain of the crowd, he brushes past the negating gaze of the individuals that compose that crowd.

He is moving forward toward zero.

II

Breughel's decline.

The miserable beyond in which he had been wallowing since Gloria Vancouver's death, as if he had to expiate that death, when nothing.

You would like to say everything at once, to evoke in the same narrative dough you knead the miasmas, insomnias, hallucination, catatonic surrender, sweat and sweat.

And the setting in which this is lived.

The domiciles of decline, you could describe several of them. The final address, Tarrafeiro Alley, is at the heart of old Macau, right next to the Inner Harbour. In a neighborhood, Patane, which Breughel stubbornly continues to call the Inner Harbour. But the place Breughel is talking about has no name. It's a shantytown built on a marsh, on Taipa, on the first of the two islands, at the foot of the New Century Hotel, right across from the hotel's luxurious sauna.

Taipa, then, but careless souls don't always notice this miniature shantytown, a shambles of shrubbery and shacks that, during the day, seems abandoned. The place's atmosphere is distressed and distressing. A network of planks zigzags across the putrid water. There are bushes, wire from an old fence, walls in corrugated metal, walls built with bricks crumbled by the damp, padlocks on the doors, smells of decomposition exhaled by a little hangar built of cinderblocks where a breeding firm has set up a henhouse and a poultry slaughterhouse.

At this time in the middle of the year of the Rooster, when Breughel chose this setting to ruminate on the end of everything, some people have a restaurant in the middle of the marsh. A hole in the wall open all night.

Garlands of vermillion bulbs light the way to the tables, and then they color the tables, the customers, the bowls of soup, at least, when it hasn't rained, when the mud hasn't risen, when the establishment isn't closed because of flooding.

Breughel has been prowling there for several weeks, tolerated by the Chinese to whom he pays daily rent and who, despite this economic relationship, pretend not to believe any proof of his existence.

He shares his space with a dog and some bottles of butane.

In the afternoon, the calm crushes the empty huts. The grass is reflected in the stagnant darkness of the gutters. You try to think of nothing, to be the grasses, their reflection. Sometimes images appear. You remember things you've read recently. In Macau, during the Japanese occupation, poverty was so abject that you could see, they say, women crouching over the sewers, picking through excrement, and crumbling the feces between their fingers to pick out what could still be consumed. There you have what your memory holds onto with no problem, that kind of information. You try to push away the ignominies of the past and those of the present. With a fixed stare, you observe the old rattan chairs thrown into the mud that the mud doesn't swallow. Nothing flows by, neither the fetid fluids nor the hours. Mosquitoes and cockroaches wait for dusk to swarm. You listen to the rumble of the trucks that. Indeed, thirty meters away, you'll find the avenue. It stretches in the direction of the village, lined with construction sites and empty lots.

In the immediate vicinity of the shanty town, there is a cemetery, an asylum for lunatics and the elderly, the university. And the New Century hotel complex, of course. You can make it out through the trees.

When night fell the fish would splash near the spot where I was trying to fall asleep: mud carps, mostly, eels, black-headed sculpin. They bubbled up in a stench of garlic and fins while, behind the fig trees, hiding the asylum from view, the lunatics moaned, making my quest for unconsciousness unlikely.

I meditated, I was going to make plans to die here, on this southern parcel of Han territory, whose purely Chinese identity had hardly been cracked by four centuries of Portuguese presence. The Portuguese were getting ready to leave, and I.

Two islands are attached to the territory of Macau: Taipa and Coloane. On Coloane lived fishermen and a leper colony. Taipa housed the madmen and the dead. Now the islands are covered with construction sites. Workers recruited in proletarian China are building graceless residences for the *nouveaux riches* of Guangdong.

Sprawled in the semi-darkness, I reflected on this extremity of space and time where some suicidal instinct compelled me to remain a foreigner falling to pieces.

Gloria Vancouver's ghost didn't visit me. Only emptiness haunted my affliction. To distract myself, I looked back on the last faces that I had met. The faces in everyday China all deserve to be contemplated with nostalgic enthusiasm, with love, but, in the streets, their gazes avoid meeting yours. I wandered among the people, wishing dully that I could transmit my admiring, begging sympathy from my eyes to theirs, and I never had the recompense of an exchange. On the sidewalks, the men denied my existence. As for the women, young and old, they went right through my body without seeing it.

For example, when I was laid out near the bottles of gas, devoured by insect bites, and I was examining the gigantic roaches scuttling in the direction of the restaurant, envying the insouciance and intellectual opacity of the cockroaches, a woman from the shantytown was approaching, with the tan face of a goddess, splendidly smooth and oval, lit up by very black eyes shaped like those of a Mongol, barely rising toward her temples. She walked by my lean-to, crushing beneath her feet the grass that marked out the perimeter of my living space, then she stepped onto the plank that led to the neighboring house and, taking no notice of me, facing toward the shadows, she belched.

Not far from there, as happened almost every evening, an animal cried out in pain.

The moaning burgeoned in the psychiatric asylum or on the hill, amongst the gray tombs, or in a farmer's hut, or near the poultry slaughterhouse, and it was so hideous that you couldn't determine what kind of beast was being tortured. In the uncertainty, one imagined sometimes a dog, sometimes a cat, sometimes a small human creature. You didn't know what. You didn't dare accept the idea that you were attending a ritual flaying, beginning again every night at the same time.

I listened to this animal's despair, and the woman passed by with a basket of laundry or food and, up above me, she belched.

III

You don't find a comfortable position, you toss and turn in the shadows. The pillow smells of gray hair, old man scalp. The smell makes you ashamed. You lie back. The bed frame creaks.

The lane is quiet. In the distance a string of firecrackers explodes, then everything is quiet again.

And you jump, startled.

Basin, night . . . dog . . . Cat! You think.

In your current abode, a shack, the bed creaks again. You sit on the edge of the warm sheets, rumpled and hot. You light a flashlight. It's four in the morning. You get up. Your bent-over silhouette can be seen moving about. You see a half-dozen cockroaches near the sink. They go about their favorite activities, which you have occasionally investigated, out of curiosity about the universe of entomologists, more than about that of the insects. You open a dictionary. Besides its odor of mildew, the paper has the texture of a sickly newspaper.

Next you can be seen shaking your head and growling. You close the book. Suddenly in the middle of the night, you'd no longer been sure of being able to draw the character—yet so simple—that means tomcat, cat, kitten, and sometimes panda, or owl, owlet. You're relieved, you sigh. You hadn't forgotten a side stroke after all.

Around the mint-green fridge and the boxes of poison, the cockroaches freeze or move about. Your sinister flashlight beam doesn't frighten them.

You come back to lie down, you turn off the light.

You dive back into insomnia.

You think about Gloria Vancouver whom only dreams and the pitiful magic of writing permit you to rejoin. And, after a few seconds, you think of Kotter. He will come, and, since he won't believe in Gloria's death, he.

He will want to hear that Gloria Vancouver is still accessible and punishable, executable. He will cling to that idea and he will strike and strike, becoming more and more single-minded and cruel. I know it will happen like that. He will have tied me to a chair and I will fall to pieces beneath the cigarette burns or blows, and I will bleat out inarticulate justifications that won't satisfy him, I will let out atrocious moans, and if, in the vicinity, any listeners happen to hear echoes of the scene, they'll ask themselves: What species of animal is that? What kind of dog? . . . Why these sobs?

And, up above me, in the presence of blood and pain, someone will belch.

IV

Kotter sets out.

Paradise has given him carte-blanche.

They finally have precise information about the place where the fugitives are hiding.

Kotter heads toward Breughel.

Now the distance that separates us has diminished.

He is rising toward the clouds.

Soon he will descend.

V

In the weeks that followed Gloria's death, I continued living in our little apartment across from the old Jetfoil Terminal.

The spot was noisy, but comfortable: bathroom, air conditioner, television.

When the loneliness of dusk destroyed all energy in me, I would turn on that machine. I would watch the weather report on a station from Hong Kong. The program was presented by a pretty girl who every night, in front of the camera, would give her name in a simultaneously childlike and captivating way—Candy Shew or Candy Siu or Candy Xiu or Candy Shiu. I liked her slight shyness, and, when her smile turned toward me, as if grazing a feeling of sadness we were the only ones to share, I noticed exquisite nuances in her voice. She had a tender tone, sweetly indecisive, for announcing the low temperatures, the relative humidity, and when a typhoon was heading toward the coast from the Philippines, her English diphthongs seemed shorter to me, more authentic, sinicized.

Flo, Gene, Becky, Lola, the feminine was used to name tropical depressions and storms, STS.

STS for Severe Tropical Storm.

Hot fog, interminably hot rains.

Showers that don't clear the air.

Noon. Everything is dripping inside the houses.

Midnight. Mushrooms bloom in the wardrobes.

The walls grow darker.

I watched, on Hong Kong TV, holdups filmed live, assaults on jewelry stores with Kalashnikovs, with grenades, nocturnal chases in ultrafast speedboats.

After the sequences showing the banditry at work, they gave the number of the response brigade. Slogans were layered on top.

JOIN FORCES AGAINST CRIME.

WE NEED OUR POLICE.

I switched off the picture, I turned off the lamps, I curled up in a corner. The ferocity of relationships between humans has always given me the passionate desire to vomit.

Sitting on the floor, at the foot of Gloria's chair, I dreamed of Gloria, murmuring anarchist phrases that she might have said at that moment or repeating pieces of dialogue that we had performed in our lifetime. Even during the thickest of our misunderstandings, even when her madness made her unrecognizable, repulsive, even then we were tuned to neighboring wavelengths. I called up Gloria Vancouver inside myself, and she came.

I closed my eyes.

For a long time, she stayed alive inside me.

On the other side of the window, uneven murmurs could be heard. The brouhaha originated from the arrival hall of the terminal, the taxi stand, the shopping mall.

In Cantonese, whether at the opera or in the street, you can often hear certain syllables suspended like a climax in the middle of certain phrases, as if the speaker, struck dumb, suddenly refused to pronounce the rest of the word or sentence. My ears would perk up and, until the small hours of the morning—because quiet never settled in—I collected these notes—high medium, falling, rising, half a step lower, half a step higher, or bass, these vowels that stretched out forever, sometimes with vehemence, rarely with languor.

I gathered them up, I found pleasure in harvesting them hour after hour, which enriched the chattering and vociferations of which I understood strictly nothing, and, for Gloria, I repeated them.

DREAM

I

You squint your eyes, little brother, your astigmatic eyes, ruined by the war and wandering, and, in the poor light, you try to read two lines written across a sheet of cardboard, a message. The message upon which your life hangs. You can't make anything out. Figures come between you and the message, a fence topped with spikes. You'll have to sneak even closer. The *chevaux de frise* creak a few meters away. Some clumsy people have gotten stuck in them and are struggling. No one is coming to help them. Soon they will be dead.

The crowd moans. Dusk is falling over the harbor. The scorching air becomes more and more yellow. The dust casts a fog over the sky in the distance, and, on the other side of the barbed wire, it turns the no-man's land saffron, with its deserted quays and buildings in ruins. Soldiers lean their backs against a truck to enjoy the spectacle offered by the rioting plebe. They're smoking, conversing. Beyond this group can be seen a triangle of dark green between two hangars.

Nothing is moving. The route leading to the islands begins there. The light is declining, but it's not the time for a romantic contemplation of the landscape. You're not watching a theatrical show, little brother, you are an actor, and your role consists in ferociously thrashing about on the concentrationary half of the stage. The set is of no aesthetic interest. You are moving about amongst eleven or twelve hundred ragged figures, bit players who look like you, sleepwalking wrecks from the dark war. Humans and animals dressed the same way. You are suffocating among the limbs and lungs. A bulletin board is the original cause of the jostling. Just on the other side of the barricade, actually, a foot soldier has tacked a piece of cardboard. The characters have been traced with a paintbrush with no thought to the calligraphy, with a cruel carelessness. You translate one of them, then another, then you're dragged off to the left by the herd. You don't know the language very well, little brother, and you need time to think about the meaning of the words, those you've managed to.

You would like to get back in front of the announcement. Vagabonds, semi-humans, and disguised animals press up against you and squeeze you. You have to protect yourself by hip checking, raising your elbows and hurting people. You have to take refuge beneath your bones. You put into practice what you know, you have learned a lot on battlefields. Around you, the breathing is raucous, like in hand-to-hand combat, gazes flee from each other. Everyone is alone. Friendship hasn't existed for ages. The tumult intensifies. Beneath your feet you feel an inert abdomen, fingers. The wall of barbed wire approaches. If someone pushed you.

If someone pushed you against it, something would happen after a few minutes of suffering that would transform you into a silhouette of meat with no future. In your own turn, after a period of spasms, you would close your hollow eyes and give up your futile gestures. And you would begin to wait.

You devote a second to reflections on the vanity of survival, but old instinctual energies flow through the core of your being, and you suddenly weigh as much as a soldier in full tactical gear, and at once you set out on an oblique trajectory, leaning into a breach in the filth with your hardened muscle. You distance yourself from the danger, you give up several decimeters to your neighbors, then several half-meters. Then you drift toward the right. Foul-smelling beings rush past you, mendicant eagles, bovines. The animals are always covered in rags.

A moment later a whirlpool movement, a vicious backwash, and, again, the ranks are pulled apart along the files. Men scream terribly then fall silent. Under the pressure of the crowd their wounds grow and they asphyxiate. They stay caught, flattened against their final resting place, embracing the spines and the bristles. Some of them collapse. You would like to touch them as little as possible, but the movement of the crowd throws you into contact with the corpses. You've returned to where you began. The distance separating you from the bulletin board is small. In order not to fall, in your turn, into the metallic barbs, you have to. You lean on a still-conscious wounded man, and as a shield against the tearing metal, you use his face, a face that is not yours and begs you. A moment goes by. The suffering of the wounded man has no limits. Your nightmare has lasted a long time and has no limits. For better or worse, you keep your balance. Emotion blinds you. Your eyes transmit a muddled picture, shot through with the bistre of dust and soot. The whole city is bellowing behind you. You notice that your mouth is open, wide open, and that, like your companions in chaos, you are howling sounds from your throat that insult the universe. Without grammar, in the general hubbub, you cry out your disgust at having to live. You are slouched, shaken, your back beaten by the furious mass, someone grabs onto you. They want to keep you from seeing, although you've finally arrived at an ideal spot to be able to read.

The light is dimming every second. Behind the soldiers' vehicle, on the charred wall of the warehouse, there is a slogan painted in white syllables on a banner.

VETERANS OF THE MANTIS'S ARMY, REGROUP!

But it is elsewhere that you.

For years you have stopped paying attention to this kind of phrase, to this vomit of the night that lies in wait. You look elsewhere, little brother.

You struggle like an illiterate, your chin jutted out toward the piece of cardboard, pupils dilated by panic.

Boat.

Six o'clock.

Islands.

Departure.

Access.

An unknown word. The idea of restriction.

Have in hand, present.

Documents.

Produce, origin, announce.

High command.

A boat will leave at six o'clock for the islands. Will only take on board holders of a pass delivered by the High Command . . .

Here ends the laborious linguistic analysis. What High Command? You didn't have the time to. The crowd tears you from your observation post, it jostles you, it pushes you far to the right, out of view of the bulletin board, it reabsorbs you, it grinds you up, and it's true that nothing can resist this brute force, but in reality that isn't what interrupted your deciphering. An internal mechanism has been set off unbeknownst to you, at the last moment, so that your eyes betray you and read the information without passing it on. You didn't want to discover the element that would mean your salvation or damnation. Because there will be no other boat, no other voyage. On your false papers is the stamp of the High Command XII of the Eastern Front, and, if this signature doesn't match that of the authority governing the port today, you'll never again have the chance to.

All around you foams a mass of acrid flesh, glistening hides and manes. You struggle bone against bone to get out of the mob. Legs knock into you and knock against you. Shirtless, his chest wet with blood, a man escorts you for the last third of a minute. From his unblinking eyes you understand that he is unconscious or dead. He totters among the dregs of all species, among all of you, he rubs up against you, doesn't manage to collapse, his face bobs about near yours, moon-shaped, impervious.

You end up speaking to this man, you sob through your closed teeth, and, all at once, you curse the dark war, the soldiers, the disguised animals, the civilians, the cadavers. No one notices any of your speech.

According to the light in the sky, it must be nine or ten o'clock.

You extract yourself from this disorder.

Now, you breathe, you rest. You inhale the smells of greasey wool, terror, and refuse that permeate the lower city. The place that you have chosen to make believe you are safe and sound is an esplanade surrounding the warehouses and an old covered market. To the south, beyond the rolls of barbed wire, sleep the jetties. Several have been damaged by bombs. The harbor master's office still dominates the oily water. The basins are motionless. Two cargo ships wait at anchor, dark, also motionless.

You are standing in front of a hangar situated to the west of the esplanade, your heart is beating, you haven't eaten for two days, a bloodstain is growing on your left hip, and, in the half-light, you read newly posted slogans.

> **PIRATES OF THE SECOND SEA, REGROUP!**
>
> **OFFICERS OF THE WOUNDED SHORES, REGROUP!**
>
> **VETERANS OF THE HIVE ARMIES, REGROUP!**
>
> **ANIMALS WITH BIG SHELLS, REGROUP!**

II

The gathering has dissipated. The destitute are getting organized for the night. The dragoons of the She-Bear regiment are coming with their bayonets to pull down the corpses lolling on the barbed wire, which, in places, made the barrier's cruelty less effective. The dragoons shake the *chevaux de frise*. Near the bulletin board, invisible in the darkness, they plunge in sharp blades, they pull them out, they replant them, they pull them out. They joke with each other in bleak tones. Then they leave once more. The corpses are now laid out in the dust. No one is walking on that side of the esplanade anymore.

You, little brother, you are walking among the improvised camps, you spy on the sparse conversations, and you finally learn what the announcement said, that much-discussed stipulation that. The High Command XII, since noon, holds the reins of local power, and it is they who control the harbor and the ships going to the islands.

The High Command XII of the Eastern Front.

You repeat that to yourself, pressing yourself against a concrete pillar. The vaguely peasant rags covering you are soaked with blood and sweat. You arrange them as well as you can, with the hope of reaching dawn without collapsing. If you had a cigarette you would smoke it in long meditative drags, listening to the dismayed recriminations and moans around you, the silences.

You imagine that you have a cigarette between your lips and you think about your falsified documents and the forger, remembering his darkened shop, his back room, his silent and fearful wife. You imagine that the smoke is enveloping your face and that you are smiling because everything is alright. In a pouch of waxed canvas, safe from the blood that from time to time runs down your left side, when the cuts reopen, you have a safe-conduct pass on the letterhead of the High Command XII of the Eastern Front, and the name of one of the heroes of the Eastern Front is stamped on your mendacious travel orders for the islands.

The forger was someone reliable, a zealot for the networks of resistance, but he proposed other seals, stamps he had already made, that he would have authenticated with signatures from captains on the general staff who seemed too precarious to you. You, little brother, gave him other names, under the influence of irrational intuitions, or because you had found them in Gloria's dreams or your own. Behind his very round glasses, the man had the piercing eyes of a raptor, one iris shot through with light brown, the other a kind of cloudy amber. He clacked his beak nervously, not stopping in his distrustful examination of your person because he sensed in you a deserter from the Regular Armies, those that had set fires to the sanctuaries of the Great-Brood, with their inhabitants and their eggs, and he hesitated between his ideological convictions and the disgust you inspired in him. You withstood his judge's stare, and, without stuttering, you pronounced the idiomatic expressions that Gloria had taught you, those words with double meanings that transmitted at once complicity and threats. You insisted: Eastern Front, High Command XII, Hong Wolguelam. Hong and no other.

You finish your cigarette.

The night is humid, stifling.

The blood is pounding in your temples, little brother. You haven't really gotten your normal breathing back. Waves of fatigue keep you off balance, by warm throbs somewhere between malaise and pain. A spike of fever is coming on. For a long time, since an offensive in the marshy area, a nasty variant of malaria has been pursuing you, and you.

You sit down against the wall of a hangar. There are fewer people than there were just a little while ago, before the episode of the poster. Some outcasts have gathered their few belongings and disappeared toward the heights overlooking the harbor. For some, hope never dies, even when the evidence of the disaster is staring them in the face. At this moment, they must be wandering among the cutthroats, looking for a hypothetical office of the High Command XII where they might get their papers modified or, at least, cry in front of someone and complain.

The esplanade is buzzing.

Groans, crashes, and tinkles that aren't always decipherable, the scraping sound of low conversation.

In one corner, refugees from the same village mark their reunion with the sound of a reed pipe incessantly repeating the same notes.

The concrete is bumpy, you can feel the fever coming on, you don't sleep, you don't trust the shadows, you think about the marauders moving with muted leaps, interrupting here and there someone's insomnia, sometimes rummaging through pockets, sometimes in between someone's collarbones, through arteries. It is dark. In the miserable damp lie those who have escaped the civil war, alone or in tiny clusters, dozing in their ethnic groups or the remains of their nationality, each one muttering in semi-consciousness, twitching. Darkness reigns over the square and there is a vast confusion of breath, rustling, worry, vigilance, silent crimes, degradation, sordid poverty.

You get up. You feel about in the space and you memorize where the corners are, in case you should have to smash an assailant up against them. You sit back down.

You shiver.

You stay motionless for a long time. You think about your trip the next day, to the islands, and Gloria's picture appears in your mind, imprecise at the beginning, so conventional that any strange woman with dark hair could replace her, then very detailed, and suddenly a magnificent portrait of Gloria appears, lit up by the light and transparency of the islands. Gloria is walking on the stones of the beach. She's not coming to meet you, but she's not getting farther away. The shore sparkles in the sun.

She exists, she doesn't exist, it's a black-haired stranger, sometimes you invent a past in which you were happy with her, a long time, a lifetime, and sometimes you didn't even speak to her, she had just brushed past you, in the clandestine apparatus whose objective was to execute those who perpetrated ethnic cleansing, arms dealers, ideologues of butchery, lords of war. Even though you are permanently tainted by war, you have remained a man who dreams his life, an inhabitant of the imagination. Without mirages you would founder, you would have foundered, you would have refused to go any farther in this hell. Gloria was walking somewhere on a coastline washed clean of all visible damage, and it was for her that you fled along mountain paths, crossing combat zones, crawling like a centipede in the nitrous-filled tunnels behind the front lines, smashing the skulls of soldier-hunters, killing and killing again one after the other, the military police who wanted to capture you and punish you horribly as a deserter. It was so that later on you could assuage your passion for her that you agreed to continue on this path, despite the wake of blood as abject as the dark war itself. Without the certainty that Gloria was waiting for you, without this amorous alliance between the two of you, the crossing of this crumbling universe wouldn't have been worth trying, and—these villainous brutish acts, you wouldn't have committed them. You would have lain down on the side of the road, on the hard, irradiated grass, and you would have turned your gun on yourself.

You hear the rasp of Gloria's steps on the stones of the beach. She is a very strange woman, very secretive, who doesn't speak much. She shakes her black hair. She stops. The waves die down near here, almost without foam. She starts walking again. She stops again, she looks at the sparkling horizon. On the other side of that line you exist, you don't exist.

At the other end of the hangar, the reed pipe sounds the same seven piercing notes one by one.

Your breathing accelerates, matches the skeletal rhythm of that tune.

Drops of sweat or humidity bead on your eyebrows.

Over your cracked lips you run your tongue with its taste of marshland. Everything is damp.

The melody doesn't change. In the darkness, around you people sigh. You get the feeling that someone lying on the ground is listening. Crawling slowly, freezing, listening. You open your eyes, two burning orbs to which blinking brings no relief. You see nothing.

You would like to forget the gnawing pain and fever that weaken you, and, all of a sudden, you are afraid of not making it through your last night on dry land. You worry about the passport and shoe thieves, and you know that some maniacs collect murders just for fun, cataloguing by the tens their knife thrusts, without any count or trophy, and that is how, from one rumination to the next, you add another kind of misfortune to these worries. At any minute, you could be denounced as a deserter, little brother, and put to death on the spot. Irascible, electrified by an unsophisticated sadism, the various military police forces don't worry about the details, whether they come from the armies of the She-Bear, companies of the Alliances, or the High Command XIII. Your false papers will have no weight if confronted with the word of a stool pigeon. Confronted with hysterical explanations. No matter how much you wave around Hong Wolguelam's signature, demonstrate that.

The mechanism is simple. A deserter alerts the police and denounces another deserter, a companion he recognizes from the field of honor. And so he ends this intolerable anxiety about escape. He is reintegrated into real life, where we find the coal braziers and villainy, and of course, he is sent to a suicide regiment where the chances of not ending up incinerated are slim, but a seed of hope is there and, at any rate, he will rejoin the close contact of the troops, so warm and unsorrowful when compared to the solitude of resistants in wartime. As for the other, the revealed fugitive, they'll drag him aside to mutilate and liquidate him.

You're afraid of that, little brother, that a former comrade from the front, hiding under civilian rags like you are, will run into you, exchange a mad stare with you, and then start bellowing your name and the common part of your registration number, until the night guard seizes you and applies the rule: **PARDON FOR YOU, DESERTER, IF YOU GIVE UP ANOTHER DESERTER!**

And so the night passes, little brother.

The flautist continues to play his monotone theme.

Mosquitoes, that flute, the heat that doesn't dissipate, and you open your eyes wide so as not to doze off and examine your living space.

Farther away you count for the thousandth time the lights that illuminate the harbor. Two torches have been lit on the other side of the *chevaux de frise*, three lamps burn on the quay, to signal the presence of water to the patrol cars. From time to time, headlights sweep over the warehouses. On one of the moored boats, there is a lantern. You count these and stay motionless against the pillar of the hangar, and you have goosebumps, your teeth are chattering, your legs stretched out on the foul ground, you reflect, you shiver, you lie in wait, shoulder blades pressing against the concrete and its hostile bumps.

Next to you are hundreds of bodies. Breathing, flatulence that. And, quite nearby, a beggar is wriggling about, sitting up in his seat, searching lengthily in the folds of his disgusting knapsack, seeking who knows what in the nothing he possesses. He strikes up a match to aid his investigation. First you see his limp pelican's beak, his feathers teeming with vermin. Then you see the silhouette of a cockroach trotting along your left leg. Then, on the wall of the hangar, you read.

**PARDON FOR YOU, DESERTER, IF YOU GIVE UP
ANOTHER DESERTER!**

And, farther away, in magnificent script, in Kordve, the common language of the chrysalids.

CHILDREN OF THE TWELFTH BANNER, REGROUP!

CHILDREN OF THE UNEXTINGUISHED MOON, REGROUP!

NYMPHS, MOTHS, NO ALLIANCE!

And, at the end, right at the moment when the flame dies down, a new slogan from the dark war:

FOR ONE UNLOVED CHRYSALID, THIRTY YEARS OF BLACK RAIN UPON YOUR DREAMS!

FICTION

Kotter doesn't have a weapon on him, because of all the security checkpoints he will have to go through to get to Macau, in the street in old Macau where Breughel lives. Nonetheless, he is obsessed with the thought of the weapon. He's never liked to threaten or kill barehanded. He digs up a meter of cord from the bottom of his pocket. He reflects on the ways he might use it on his Asian mission. During the trip's many hours, he twists this about and contemplates it instead of sleeping.

The landing in Hong Kong is preceded by a flyover of the Guangdong coast, with its inlets and islands, its islets, hundreds of them. The panorama echoes exactly the information given by the guidebooks Kotter consulted before leaving. No condensation remains on the plane's window. The morning light illuminates China. You can see everything.

Kotter looks.

The airplane slows down above several port complexes. Since it doesn't yet have authorization to land, it is flying in circles. The boats are milling about. Trawlers, barges, floating cranes, tugboats, ferries.

At this height it would be dishonest to pretend to be able to differentiate clearly between junks and police speedboats. Kotter notices the junks.

The sea has an undefinable color, a deep green of paralyzing beauty. Words are incapable of. You search in vain. Something very intense sticks in your memory forever. Later on you will run your finger down a list of stones, on the "Minerals and Fossils" plate in an encyclopedia, but nothing matches it. Chrysolites and jadeites awaken no emotion, and, without finishing, you close the book. You have to admit that, in this field as well, vocabulary has its shortcomings.

Then the airplane sweeps down through the houses.

The fuselage that careens at three hundred kilometers per hour between the buildings of Kowloon.

The air conditioners jutting out of the façades of the towers.

Closed windows, and behind them, in a flash, you get a bit of Chinese family bric-à-brac, with fleshy plants, old cardboard boxes, bird cages, bottles of oil, and red plastic containers.

The taxis—also red.

Then suddenly touchdown on the runway surrounded by water.

Bounded by a water still inexpressibly green.

After turning around, the plane rolls slowly toward dry land.

Giant advertisements for Marlboro, Kent.

In the cabin you begin to breathe the unfiltered air from outside, a rotten humidity whose insipidity surprises Kotter.

The smell of a poorly maintained laundry.

Then, waiting in line. Half an hour in one spot before you get to the desk of the border guards. Then a completely unlikeable NCO stamps a visa on Kotter's passport. A nametag de-anonymizes the man.

LAM KAM C. has authorized Kotter to enter the colony's territory.

To get to Macau from Hong Kong, explains Kotter's research, the traveler must go to the Macau Ferry Terminal. Several types of transportation compete at this point whose respective advantages are hard to discern, as his research didn't recommend one rather than the other. Jetfoil, SuperShuttle, highspeed ferry. Everything looks good.

Kotter buys a Jetfoil ticket.

For the second time that morning, he waits in front of an immigration official. A certain **NG CHONG**, who types on an invisible keyboard. As the screen tells him that Kotter hasn't broken any laws in Hong Kong during his brief stay, he makes no commentary. Under the stamp permitting entry, he affixes a seal legalizing his exit.

Then Kotter embarks.

It's a radiant day.

Now Kotter is gliding over the calm water. He zigzags between trawlers. He flies along the deserted shoreline.

He floats on the surface of very green and very calm waters, never knowing if he is really sailing over the China Sea, or if he's dreaming.

After an hour and a quarter, the jetfoil diminishes the speed of its motor and maneuvers into the port of Macau called the Outer Harbour. He disembarks.

The dampness overwhelms Kotter when he leaves the refrigerated space of the boat. Scarcely has he set foot on the dock when the new smell of a communal laundry welcomes him, the odors already detected after landing in Kowloon. He breathes in a powerful gulp of exotic humus. His nostrils flare with no distress. He is thinking of nothing. He has acclimated.

Barriers channel the surge of humanity from the gangway to the border checkpoint. Few conflicts are visible, and the crowd doesn't seem aggressive, but in reality, everyone is pushing everyone.

Colonial ceiling fans are fulfilling, above their heads, their symbolic function, stirring up more nostalgia than fresh air.

An eruption of tiny drops of sweat torments Kotter. He lifts the crook of his arm to wipe his forehead. Behind the plate-glass windows of the hall, the sea looks yellower, muddier than in Hong Kong.

A girl in uniform stamps Kotter's papers.

Kotter has always appreciated women. With pleasure he examines the round, slight face, agreeable but lacking any smile or even any hint of a smile. When he takes his passport back, he says thank you in Mandarin, two syllables easy to memorize and pronounce, one of the words he had managed to retain as he was preparing his mission at home, with headphones on his ears. He thanks the form, the face. At the same time, he makes a note of the girl's name.

KWOK F. in black letters on brushed aluminum.

Flora, maybe? Fanny?

He is hoping for a glimmer from her, some movement of approval. There was, all the same, on his side, a proof of cultural goodwill. He hopes at least for a blink of her eyes. But F. doesn't react, doesn't answer, doesn't light up.

Then, through the crowd Kotter goes.

In front of the doors of the hall, an employee of the Westing Resort hotel turns toward him a sign on which it says: **WELCOME DUPONT**.

The employee stares at Kotter, inspecting his plausibly Dupont appearance. Kotter makes a negative sign. Between the two men, for a fraction of a second, floats a sensation of failure.

The heat is infernal. Beneath Kotter's jacket, a canvas windbreaker bought in a catalogue, drops of sweat are erupting. The catalogue extolled the lightness of the cloth, the many pockets. Underneath it the sweat erupts and forms larger drops. With a handkerchief Kotter mops off his eyes, forehead, mouth.

Then a taxi takes him to the west of the city, in the direction of the Inner Harbour where he knows Breughel lives. The driver wants to avoid traffic jams. He takes the coast road, passing palaces with no personality and construction sites.

On the other side of the water, now yellow, brown, *café au lait*, Taipa has nothing particularly picturesque, and there is no one on the sidewalks here, almost no one. Kotter's vaguely touristic preconceptions are falling apart. He gives up on exploring the landscape and its ambiance. He relaxes in the glacial cold inside the car. Under the transparent vinyl covering the seats there are white embroidered chrysanthemums. Near the rearview mirror dangles a little garland made of vermillion trinkets with gold coins, a portrait of Mao. The radio plays Canto-pop.

Kotter flips through his passport. He glances at the stamp from Flora or Fanny Kwok's hands.

The visa is good for three weeks.

A miserly length.

But long enough, thinking of the Vancouver-Machado-Breughel file, to tie up the loose.

Quite enough.

MONOLOGUE

Pleasantries were exchanged, as always in such cases, and without sitting down on one of the two available chairs, or on the edge of the bed I said You really live at the ends of the earth, then I said If you want to call me Kotter that much, we can go ahead with Kotter, I don't see any problem, Smith would have worked just as well but Kotter fits me like a glove, then I say My name isn't important, what matters is that I'm sent by Paradise, you know what that means, right, then I said Paradise or the Party, there too we can agree on a name, I'm not a stickler about the label, then After several years of calm you maybe thought we'd given up tracking you, that we had gotten discouraged, and I added But in fact, no, then I smiled at Breughel and said to him with a rather pensive tone, Because we are persistent, Breughel, terribly persistent, then, anticipating an aggressive movement from Breughel, I put my arm out and hit Breughel in the mouth, with abrupt violence, as I know how to do, as I was taught in the training centers, and Breughel, who had attended jiu-jitsu dojos in his youth, tried to grab my elbow, but he didn't have the time to dodge a second blow and he moaned and backed toward the bed hiding the bottom half of his face, he hid behind his forearm like a deceitful child afraid of punishment, and at that moment I saw that he was going to slide his hand between the bedframe and the mattress, doubtlessly meaning to pull out a weapon from its hiding place, a knife or revolver, and I rushed over and said Come on now no funny business, and I brought his carpals and metacarpals up behind his shoulder blades, forcing him to adopt a crippled posture, bent over and submissive, then I led him to the nearest chair, then I reached into the left inside pocket of my jacket and took out a remarkable replica of a Smith & Wesson M39 that I had found in a toy store a hundred meters from the shack where Breughel lived, and I brandished this object saying It's no good, Breughel, and then I said, don't make things difficult, don't make me, and, while I pointed the excellent imitation of a black muzzle at him, aiming at his kneecaps or thighs, because blowing his brains out was out of the question at this stage of the investigation, I rifled under the mattress with my left hand, first finding nothing but an envelope full of patacas and Hong Kong dollars, then beneath that I fished out a wallet containing a passport and another bundle of dollars, and finally wrapping my fingers around an unloaded pistol, it looked like a Belgian Browning, an FN-Browning 1910, but later turned out to be unidentifiable, made in a Vietnamese armory, maybe, or in a clandestine workshop of the Fujian mafia, and I said I could break one of your bones to show you that I'm not kidding, Breughel, but I'm sparing you, and I added Cooperate, you won't get hurt, a phrase which had been used as a password at the time when Breughel, without being a Party agent, still had good relations with the Party, at the time when he had the status of fellow traveler and when he wasn't yet mixed up with trying to hide Gloria Vancouver from the Party police, then I opened the passport, which looked exactly like an official document, apart from its authenticity, and, after examining the mournful photo of Breughel, I read aloud the details he had provided to the forger: Mattias Goetz, born December 9, 1947, in Rio de Janeiro, Brazil, then I said This must have cost you an arm and a leg, and as he didn't answer I leaned against the door of his hut, a panel of iron pierced by a barred transom through which the daylight filtered sparsely, and I confiscated the miserable booklet with its wine-colored cover that conferred Portuguese citizenship on its bearer, not very popular in general, but here the most natural and least suspicious, and in another pocket I stored the Fujian pistol and I said, You'll tell me, when the time comes, where you keep the cartridges for this little wonder, and as he indicated to me a rather large geographical area with a morose hand movement, he situated the hiding place somewhere between the books and the clothes piled on the floor, I said Soon Goetz, when the time comes, there's no hurry, then I wiped the sweat dripping down my eyelids and my cheeks and I said Your lips are covered in blood, clean yourself off, and, while he dabbed at his lips with a dirty handkerchief, I considered him without emotion, suddenly a little shocked to have ended up here, in this dark room, 22°16′ latitude N and 113°35′ longitude E, and to have so easily been able to get the upper hand on Gloria Vancouver's companion, an individual of great resources, an obscure writer, dangerous and unpredictable, claimed one of the records concerning him, and, while the drops of respiration re-formed on my face, I let out a theatrical sigh and exclaimed You could have hidden out somewhere else besides the tropics all the same, then I said, because my jacket, although designed for tourism in hot countries, was sticking to my shoulders and sides, I wonder how you manage to hold up with no air conditioning, and, after walking to the fridge and trying in vain to turn on the fan sitting on top of it, I added With no air conditioning or anything, then I felt myself overcome with a brief but imperious desire to lie down and be quiet, by a vertigo I had to attribute to the jet lag, to the lack of sleep over the fifteen hours of airplane travel, and also to the fact that I hadn't stopped rushing about since landing in Kowloon, hurtling in a taxi from the airport to the Macau Ferry Terminal with the idea that I would be able to relax on the Hong Kong–Macau trip, but then not managing to get rest on the jetfoil, dozing between two Chinese women inhaling noodles served in disposable cardboard bowls, then nibbling pieces of grilled cuttlefish, falling asleep for a few seconds at a time then waking up, assaulted at each moment by the bleating announcements proposed by the loudspeakers in Cantonese, then in English, then in Portuguese, sometimes for duty-free cigarettes, sometimes for lottery tickets, sometimes instructions to follow in case of shipwreck, then since the moment I arrived, setting off in search of a place to crash not far from Breughel, then having taken a shower in a room at the Peninsula Hotel, not losing a single quarter- or half-hour contemplating the old port, the floating casino, and China, or lying down on the bed with my eyes closed and my mind shut off, without losing time going to Breughel's place, to the address where we had learned he had gone to earth, apparently alone, and, after having acquired a plastic Smith & Wesson M39, looking first for Tarrafeiro Street, then Tarrafeiro Alley, a kind of sordid corridor between houses arriving at the final stages of dilapidation, to finally have the door open and to push Breughel into his lair and start a conversation with him, and, while the pitching and rocking grew stronger inside my skull, I growled Spill it, Breughel, so we can get it over with, then I said, as I always say to lower the drama of the atmosphere, Let's go over it   from the very beginning, but Breughel shrugged his shoulders and grumbled, I don't understand what you want, Kotter, leave me alone, and he crossed his arms and began to furrow his brow, staring obstinately at the upside-down chair, because, in the short scuffle that had occurred, the second chair had fallen over along with the clothes it held, a pair of canvas pants and a denim jacket, as well as undergarments on the verge of deterioration, and, as he was displaying the intention not to unclench his teeth, at least in the immediate future, I went back to the door and turned the key, and after righting the chair, I sat down on it, picking up only the jacket and searching it, listing the results of my search in a low voice, A few patacas, two felt-tip pens, a ticket for a Chinese opera, a black and red notebook, several illegible receipts, and, having finished my inventory, I asked Breughel You like Chinese opera, but he didn't express himself on the subject and, whimpering, applied the dubious wad of his handkerchief to his gums, above all to emphasize my cruelty and the human rights violations of which he had been the victim, and I began to leaf through the red and black notepad, naturally wishing to discover in it something to do with Gloria Vancouver or Machado, a note, a reference, a telephone number, and I said Listen, Breughel, we're not going to play cat and mouse, that would be a waste of adrenaline, useless tension for both of us, and, after a pause, I said You know why I'm here, so talk, and he hissed through his teeth, creating a sound that brought to mind neither a cat nor a mouse but rather a grass snake, a badly off grass snake, and then he murmured You'd think we were in a bad spy novel, and I retorted Why bad, and, as he had returned to his obstinate attitude, I temporarily lost interest in his pouting and scanned a few pages of the notebook, immediately noticing that they formed a series of drafts of vignettes destined, doubtless, to make up a novel or something like that, and I read for example These Chinese women passing by, walking with faces full of magical harmonies, crossing paths day and night with Breughel, in the streets, in the shops . . . all the places where Breughel walks . . . cemeteries too . . . these girls who never meet Breughel's gaze for more than one hundredth of a second . . . or again, on the back of the same page, The many black variations of their black hair . . . at the university library, the students who fold their arms up for a pillow . . . and who sleep . . . under that brilliant unfurled mass . . . , and I skipped several sentences like this and read It was then long beyond death . . . for the two of us . . . and, on the following page, strange surrealist slogans, like FOR ONE SCRATCHED CHRYSALID, SEVEN SAILORS CHARRED TO THE MARROW! Or, later on, INFANTA OF THE NINTH BANNER, MAKE CONTACT WITH THE PIRATES! then I lifted my eyes toward Breughel and asked him if he was writing a new book, and if we had here the raw material that he meant to, but Breughel interrupted me, calling me Kotter again, and he made a gesture like that of a man refusing a fight and he said Let me die, Kotter, then he said I have nothing more to, and, after catching his breath, he added You've come much too late, Kotter, Machado and Gloria have left this world, now I want to curl up and wait, my life is over, Kotter, I want nothing more than that, to curl up and wait. Let me.

LOGBOOK

I

I had so often described my confrontation with Kotter that I no longer knew whether Kotter really existed, with his plastic pistol and his cord, and if the interrogation had taken place at some point or if it might still happen, or if Kotter existed only inside Breughel's addled brain—that is to say, in mine.

I abruptly sat up in the darkness and pushed off the shroud under which, for hours.

I sit up in the darkness, I push off the sheets fouled by an anxious heat and, as in the past, in Gloria's time, when Gloria stammered nightmares next to me and sobbed, I listened.

The nights here have always been exhausting.

In Tarrafeiro Alley nothing is moving, silence has fallen, but, beyond that, the Chinese city buzzes and buzzes, incapable of experiencing anything but broken sleep, divided into multiple attempts interrupted carelessly by distant bellows, calls, then the indecent clamor of a television set, the whine of a saw attacking metal, and then the murmur and clinking of a meal being eaten, or the blows of a hatchet on a chopping block cutting up black market pork, or the maneuvers of a pickup truck in front of a shop, then the crisp detonation of a pack of firecrackers that a lucky or unlucky gambler has lit upon leaving a gaming room, in front of the floating casino or elsewhere, then the siren of a police ambulance.

I could turn the lights on, study a little Chinese, relearn the characters I've forgotten since dozing off an hour earlier. I could also open one of my notebooks and write a few sentences about the Party, about Paradise, about Gloria, or write a new version of one of Gloria's dreams, or continue to invent episodes of my fight with Kotter.

But I stay still, swallowing with neither strength nor pleasure the stifling air of the bedroom, the gas so poor in oxygen and so rich in parasites and germs.

I wait.

Every ten minutes, the refrigerator's motor switches on.

I float in the black space, my ear passively on alert, my body dull, defenseless. I listen to the night around me, the night of the Inner Harbour, I remember other nights like this, and I wait.

II

Gloria's whimpers collided with my unconscious. I jumped.

I emerged.

Gloria, in her sleep, panted pleadingly. Her nightmare had already lasted several minutes. I heard her stammer a speech of which not one word was understandable, then she was quiet, as if to permit an interlocutor to formulate a question, then she responded again with explanations in a thick voice. Her breathing calmed, accelerated, calmed again. Her hands shook.

When she reached the brink of a scream I took her in my arms,

I wrapped her up, I tried to erase with simple gestures the horrible images that visited her. Her skin was becoming coarse. I caressed her shoulders. I stroked the curve of her hip.

Sometimes she would wake up. She avoided my gaze in the half-light. She was panting, she pulled away from me with a bitterness I found insulting. She didn't tell me what she had just been through, what ordeals.

She no longer told me her dreams.

The light of signs near our window drew on us and the ceiling, blue stripes and pink or mauve triangles.

Damp and naked, Gloria sat on the edge of the bed. Her back was to me. She was now breathing evenly, sniffling from time to time.

Can I do anything for you? I asked.

Outside you could hear the jetfoil starting out for Hong Kong. People were talking in front of a restaurant door. It wasn't late. One o'clock, one-thirty.

Gloria's hair formed a very dense black mass, well kempt despite the circumstances. For a second, nothing kept me from imagining that.

I imagined that another woman sat there, just as unsociable, and in Gloria's place a daughter of the Han pouted, mute, petrified by the disappointment after her experience with a foreign devil, come to marry me on a whim, and now, reflecting on the best way to get herself repudiated without losing face. Then the confusion dissipated. The daughter of the Han had disappeared. Gloria was speaking.

She was speaking, reeling off sentences in a purposely disembodied voice, but her words were constantly choked and hoarse. She had to clear it by coughing.

She wanted to go back to the islands, to make contact with the Party again, to pay back the amount she had stolen, to separate from me, she knew very well, besides, that I couldn't stand living in her company anymore, she was going to try to find Machado, who wasn't dead, she wouldn't hesitate to go to him as soon as he signaled. Machado wasn't dead, no, he was traveling, and traveling in the direction of the islands. Then she announced that she intended to opt for Chinese citizenship at the end of the century, when the People's Republic would replace the Portuguese. She would be Chinese, she would master the language, she would be part of a theater troupe, a neighborhood troupe of amateurs. Or she would ask me to organize for us as quickly as possible a week of vacation in Taiwan, the Philippines, Thailand, just for a change of air. She was suffocating. Because of me, mostly, because of the obstacle I represented in her life, she was suffocating.

Then we were both quiet.

We were dripping with sweat.

We never plugged the air conditioner in at night, so as not to be deprived of the constant murmurs emerging in front of the arrival and departure halls of the jetfoil, and also because we doubtlessly liked to sleep and not sleep leaving the window ajar, in the middle of the mosquitoes, in the middle of the human voices, surrounded by water, by boat and bus fuel, in the smells of the people and their food and their lives.

What's the matter, for you to be looking at me like that, Gloria said suddenly, you'd think you've never seen anything, that you've never seen a madwoman.

III

In a tiny nameless road of Patane I saw an octogenarian urinate into a tin can.

I saw in Kong Cheong Street a poultry farmer who slaughtered astonished, fatalistic chickens one after another, and then threw them into a blue plastic barrel.

In Guangzhou I saw a man strangle a woman on the Yanjiang Quay, on the bank of the Pearl River.

In that same Pearl River, on the same Yanjiang Quay, I saw, floating near the surface, the corpse of a peasant woman.

At Coloane I saw a leper missing half his face.

I saw a Chinese man in an overcoat bet, on a single card, the equivalent of 150 years of a proletarian's salary in Shanghai.

In the Tam Kong temple in Coloane, I saw opera actors pay homage to divine idols by playing the drum and flute for them.

I saw barefoot workmen swing from a bamboo perch on top of a thirty-story building.

During a typhoon I saw corrugated metal fences soaring over construction sites.

I've witnessed a cemetery catch fire, I've seen fire break out in an old firecracker factory.

I saw firemen pulling the legs of a dismembered woman out of a dumpster.

So go ahead and tell me I've seen nothing.

IV

A gust of wind runs through Tarrafeiro Alley, then into the void. Something falls, a metallic object. Half a bicycle wheel from the 1950s or a very old air conditioner cover. It falls in front of the red altar at the dead end of the alley.

In the bedroom where almost nothing can be made out, Breughel stays sitting for a long time. He opens his eyes wide, unable to say whether he feels like going back to bed. The horribly rumpled sheets won't be untangled before dawn, the mattress won't cool off. Breughel meditates on the edge of the bed, his feet on a sheet of newspapers. His breath is audible. Sometimes he stops breathing, as sometimes happens with the seriously depressed. Deprived of oxygen, he scrutinizes the night. Drops of sweat roll down his chest, sometimes burning, sometimes cold, nervous.

Then, on Gloria's suggestion, we went to Korea for a few days, he thinks. In South Korea, in Seoul.

Then he gets up.

He feels along the wall, finally finding the light switch. What springs from the lightbulb sprays the space with raw light. You'd think you were on a theater stage, in a set showing a leftist's lair a thousand years before the global revolution. The rays hit Breughel's desolate grimace, then bounce back to the packing crates serving as furniture, leaving gloomy shadows behind them.

Breughel goes to the sink, toward the hotplate.

He avoids the small table where plates, bowls, the typewriter, and sheets of paper coexist.

We can see a folder lying there that we would like to see Kotter dive into, instead of mistreating Breughel while demanding revelations from him about Gloria Vancouver. But we also know how vain the trouble Breughel went to was when he wrote, when he copied stories down for Kotter on paper, responses to. In the hope that he would succeed in redirecting Kotter's thoughts onto background subjects and that, finally, he would foil his criminal plans. We know how illusory this task is, because the killer, even if he skims a few lines, a few paragraphs, won't read them.

I am writing for a reader who wants to destroy me, for a reader who doesn't know my work and won't even open my book, the fragments of my books, thinks Breughel.

But what does it matter, he goes on thinking.

His hand extends toward the shelf above the sink.

Next to a tablet of anti-cockroach poison canned goods and packets of food are lined up. We can see, for example, instant desserts, sweet soup that you can boil in a bag in five minutes.

Coconut milk sago, a green can.

Almond cordial with mushrooms, a blue can.

Green beans with kelp, an orange can.

Breughel fills a pot with water. He lights the gas.

Like this, he keeps turning his own thoughts or Kotter's away onto minor, terribly secondary details.

Now in the pot an aluminum pouch of soybeans and a few strips of kelp boil.

A second gust of wind drives back into the room the odors of detritus from the Inner Harbour.

The door shakes.

The weather is changing.

V

Then we went to Korea, to Seoul, and I came back alone.

FICTION

There were several gusts of wind at the end of the night, and then the day broke, torrid, with no breeze.

I had dozed off around five o'clock. I stood up, respecting the slowness my body demanded, like a zombie coming back from its long voyage in the abyss.

Inside the walls the boiling heaviness of the morning was already fermenting. Crushed by the leaden remains of the night, you can perceive around you an extra hint of fetidity, a little hint. You can feel the molecules reluctantly penetrating your nasal cavity. In your skull the daily fog is taking shape again. You would like to be done with it all, to be finally abstract, to leave your spongy matter, the exhausted and spongy world of bodies.

I would rediscover my body.

I went to the tap, I took off my briefs and.

Breughel undressed in front of the sink, and he washed himself from head to foot. The tepid water from the tap splattered the ground covered with newspapers. *South China Morning Post*, *Herald Tribune*, *A Tribuna de Macau*. The Hong Kong radio spat the exchange rates out into the shadows, as well as news of the quarrel between Beijing and London about the future airport. Things seemed to be getting worse. An alarmist had dug up an old hawkish article by Deng Xiaoping, written ten years earlier, and, at the moment when Breughel was soaping between his legs with that pensive brusqueness that characterizes people who live alone, the governor Chris Patten was yet one more time being sarcastic about the goodwill of the Chinese faction. Chris Patten's English was a model of Oxford perfection. The negotiations were courting rupture, as they often did.

Of the tropical storm I knew was hovering for the last forty-eight hours to the Northeast of the Philippines, no news.

Breughel then swallowed a bowl of rice porridge and two sausages. He had changed the station. You could hear a Canto-pop singer singing about lovesickness, then two journalists chattered in Cantonese. I think they were rereading the stock tips from the day before. In a low voice, to keep his ear in, Breughel repeated a few numbers. I didn't catch anything else.

I had always wanted to make progress in the local language, but Gloria wasn't there anymore to teach me what she'd gleaned at the market or in the street. As for self-teaching manuals, they couldn't agree on the basic phonetic facts, which, from the first lesson, had a tendency to.

Examples:

There are basically 6 tones in Cantonese.

There are 7 tones in Cantonese.

There are 9 tones in the Cantonese dialect.

After having dispensed with some of my bitterness on that subject, I dedicated five minutes to a cursory tidying-up. I had opened the door to air out the room. On the threshold was a dead roach, frozen in a natural pose, yes, but defunct. I pushed it out of the way.

There was no one else in the tiny street.

The sky was shining between the roofs too high to affect the atmosphere near the ground. At the end of the cul-de-sac, the altar might very well have been recently coated with vermillion, it didn't change anything either. A stick of incense smoked in the niche of painted bricks, charming the local demon. Insensitive to this delicate attention, the demon rolled its furious eyes.

Sometimes I'll light incense sticks in front of idols. For me it is a way of thinking very hard about Gloria. In these moments of feigned piety, I remember Gloria who gathered information about Chinese superstitions, popular rituals, divination, offerings, and who, when she visited on old temple, threw into the coals a bundle of bills from the Hell Bank, denominations of fifty million dollars she had just bought from the caretaker for three patacas. Like Gloria, but with my mind filled with nostalgia, with the image of absent Gloria inside me, I imitate the pious, preferably in front of grotesque or terrifying gods. I dare do this and I dare do it without shame. I brandish a bouquet of smoking prayers. I wave them in front of my respectfully bowed forehead. Then I stick them upright in the sand mixed with ashes.

At this instant, Mrs. Fong cracked a door open and threw out a bunch of floor sweepings toward a neighboring puddle; among them could be seen a fish head, a fish of respectable size, like a carp. Nearly a bucketful immediately went to feed the puddle.

The water was an inky mirror with hints of anthracite and an incandescent sheen made of fat and oil. The fish head came to rest on one cheek, it didn't even bother to gulp down the reflection of the flies that approached it; it seemed disgusted with everything.

The day wasn't so loathsome, though, because I remembered how to write ink, fly, fish, head.

This day, at any rate, was continuing.

Breughel was already locking the door of his shack.

He shook the iron panel to make sure that the lock held, then, skirting the trash bins that crowded the sidewalk on the corner of Tarrafeiro Street, he left Tarrafeiro Alley.

Immediately he rejoined the world, the brouhaha, the crowd, the colorful smells, the intolerable heat, the black-haired figures, the gazes that never lingered on him, the omnipresent inscriptions.

The Han writing.

The signs everywhere sung above our heads in a Sino-Portuguese mixture I hadn't gotten tired of yet. His gaze flitted from one to the other, paused. He ventured out every day with renewed pleasure.

KAM POU, CAFÉ.
ARTIGOS ELECTRICOS SUN KAI.
BICICLETAS I LEI.
FARMACIA CHUN CHEONG.
LIVRARIA HO TAI.
LEI IAN WENG, DENTISTA.
MAESTRE DE MEDECINA CHINESA LOU WENG IO.
MA HENG HONG, CAFÉ.

Now he was passing groups of high school students in green uniforms jostling around the kettles of a food cart, counting their patacas, and hesitating vehemently between the dishes offered: skewers of octopus, red with chili or plain violet, skewers of mussels, of sausage, skewers of white tripe, duck quarters in steaming broth.

Right next to them, on a woman's back, a baby turned its face up toward Breughel and contemplated me with dreamy fixedness.

With time, and if his mother hadn't intervened to put his thoughts and atlas in order, I know that we would have been able to establish contact, the beginning of a contact.

But now, nothing.

LIVRARIA, VAP SAN.
LAM NGAN VUN, DENTISTA.
KONG SOU CHAN, DENTISTA.

For hours, Breughel walked at random. Sometimes he thought about Gloria. Sometimes sweat blinded him. He could be seen working to isolate exotic details and memorizing them so that he could later fill out the texts he was fabricating for Kotter with them.

Ruled by the obsessive certainty that one day Kotter would come and read them. And that they would lead him astray.

A few examples.

Dishwashing behind restaurants. Between the plastic pipes and trashcans, squatting women move around tubs of murky water. Handfuls of chopsticks laid on the asphalt, on piles of dirty bowls.

On the rotisserie gallows, the glazed ducks proliferate, and on the neighboring hooks hang the tortured victims who have suffered various outrages. Flattened ducks, round ducks, condemned to another sentence than that of a glaze. Smashed. Transformed into a cadaverous crepe with a beak.

Farther on, two men are killing eels. They kill them between their feet, on tiptoe, then they slit them lengthwise. The gesture of a card player followed by a spasm. Then some additional surgery. That's where food begins.

The place is dripping in red.

Then we detour around a man in a shirt and tie frozen in the middle of everything, holding forth on his cell phone.

Now we're crossing a covered market.

The stifling stench of henhouses and black space, cement, unlighted stalls, mildew on dark pillars.

So-called hundred-year-eggs, still covered in the earth where they have aged for weeks.

The basins full of feathers, entrails.

The liquids of carnage that flood the ground, the black rubber snakes from which spurt invading water.

Everyone is mired down near the ground, with the exception of fish kept in agony on metal displays.

The sound of cutting and deboning. The Chinese knives shaped like cleavers. The jostling of containers. Often enough the hardy voices of the working women ring out. Rasping final vowels, middle tones lacking any goodwill.

An old woman dozes in a corner. Everyone moves about in a crouch in the offal. The women in black pants. Remember the images in case you ever have to swallow something other than vegetal. It's all there, consumables and consumers. In woven reed cages or metal fish traps, the chickens are red and waiting.

Breughel reemerges into the open air.

Then he is standing in a bus heading for Taipa.

Underneath the bridge float skiffs loaded with sand.

In the bus, a baby with downy eyelashes notices Breughel's eyes on him and he turns away abruptly.

But, anyway.

For the moment I had gathered enough notes to slake Kotter's thirst for things out of the ordinary.

The fiction could begin again, that is to say, my life.

I found myself now on Taipa, on the other side of the branch of the sea separating Macau from its islands, and I was looking out the bus window at the yellow waves curling below the road, slowly dying on the seawall, leaving very little foam on the rocks, with a softened slowness. The stones themselves struck me with their extremely yellow color. The waves weakly licked the visible roots of the pines stretched out over the mud, the wet sand, it went all the way to the debris that had landed there during the last typhoon, half a canoe torn from the boat club, an advertisement panel for cigarettes, Kent, I think. Then the bus braked violently in front of a corrugated metal shelter, and I was thrown toward the outside furnace in the company of a woman who worked at a casino, recognizable by her lilac uniform, and of three high school students, also in uniform, white.

I was in the habit of getting out there rather than across from the shantytown. That allowed me to make sure no one had followed me. I had taken that precaution, without missing a single time, since the middle of the year before, the date when Gloria had been admitted to the psychiatric services of the asylum. I could under no circumstances let Kotter learn the truth about Gloria Vancouver. I couldn't let him learn the truth or even suspect that Gloria was still alive, shut up with the insane and locked in her own personal universe, but physically vulnerable, always accessible to mortal brutality and suffering.

I never stopped thinking of Gloria and of the best way to protect Gloria from Paradise, the Party, from the possible eruption of Kotter into our. Into what was left of our existence.

Totally unreceptive to human sadness, several thousand Chinese locusts stridulated near the bus stop, hidden in the ragged weeds of the median or in the underbrush of the hill that rose in a steep slope on the south side of the road, or perched on the branches of trees whose names I didn't care for or didn't know, Asiatic varieties that cast shadows with no depth. This deafening insect song covered the noise of the tractor trailers changing gears around the corner, near the Hyatt hotel. It was a hymn to the glory of the great heat. It was born at dawn and its enthusiasm would not wane before dusk.

I caught my breath in the shade of what looked like a weeping willow. I felt like I was being cooked. The veins swelled in my temples. I was alone. No suspicious shadows were prowling in the vicinity. The high schoolers had evaporated, the lilac dress disappeared into a service entrance in one of the Hyatt's buildings. No one was walking on the side of the road.

For the moment I was there, up against the bark, breathing like a sick mammal.

Under the superb arch of the Taipa bridge passed junks, barges, small trawlers flying red flags.

Macau gleamed white on the other side of the still sea.

In the Outer Harbour, a jetfoil arrived.

I shook myself, I crossed the road, the intersection. I walked past the Hyatt's parking lot and casino, then headed to the shantytown.

Between the shacks and the putrid ditches, nothing had changed since the day before. The bird cages were in their place, the bindweed and groundcover spread over the old batteries and broken chairs, among the scavenged containers, colorless tarps, bottles of gas, wire, warped corrugated metal, low walls of cinder blocks, tiles touched by leprosy or blight, worn-out baskets, cardboard boxes, utility poles, holes full of stagnant water, slabs of cement forming here and there precarious paths, between rows of planted onions, beds of Chinese cabbage, the red lightbulbs that at night illuminated the way to the restaurant, the ropes and hooks for drying clothes, the pools of dark blue mud, the barrels of light blue plastic, incomprehensible posters.

But I didn't stop. Already I was walking in the shadow of the New Century Hotel, protected from the sun by the mass of the sauna. The path to the asylum is barely two hundred meters long and has no charm. On the left, white walls rise up, behind which can be imagined pharaonic opulence, with sleazy swimming pools where hostesses in bath towels and masseuses stroll, and, on the right, you have the dregs of the fourth world.

The sauna's vents spat out steam.

On the other side of the marsh, on the construction sites, pile-drivers rammed stakes into the ground.

A dog joined me and escorted me to the asylum's gate, then turned around. There was no one in the guard box. I passed through the entrance.

The old people paid me no attention and continued to ruminate on their cement or plastic seats. The mad people, on the other hand, were curious at seeing me. In no way disdainful, some approached to greet me. We had tamed each other over the last months, almost years. When I am talking about the mad people, I am not talking about all the sick people, of course. I'm talking about the men who came toward me with great friendship. They accepted my existence and, without distaste, unlike the non-interned Chinese, touched me. They were dressed according to the traditions of asylum fashion: t-shirts, shorts, sandals, and they would touch me. They were all thin.

As I always did, I began to exchange with them a gesticulated commentary about the food, President Mao, the real estate speculation disfiguring the territory, about a bird with a loud and raucous cry that would often perch on the top of a fig tree in the senile patients' courtyard.

Our language was a fraternal pantomime. I imitated the bird, its call. I babbled commonplaces in Mandarin, with no concern about making myself understood. I accompanied with sounds the happiness of being together and describing the world held in common.

We were all suffering from the heat, but, except for me, no one was sweating.

A nun exited the schizophrenics' wing and crossed the courtyard.

She was a Filipina with a coarse face. She smiled from behind unflattering glasses. Her arrival had the effect of dispersing the small group surrounding me. I appreciated this woman, with whom I had frequently had occasion to chat, and who sincerely believed that Gloria's condition would improve with time. She babbled a little in English, speculating on the typhoon threatening the territory, then led me to Gloria's room.

Gloria's individual, air-conditioned room.

If we come right down to it, this is what, now, the fortune stolen from Paradise was being used for: guaranteeing for Gloria, in the decrepit psychiatric hospital of Taipa, decent conditions of internment.

Gloria stood, apathetic, in front of the window. She was fixing her empty gaze on the branches of the tall trees. I touched her hair lightly. She shrugged her shoulder and pushed away from this beginning of an embrace.

I'm here, I said.

Ah, she said.

She went to sit on the bed.

Some locks of hair fell in front of her eyes. She didn't brush them away. I tried to do it for her. She now accepted my presence next to her. I didn't force her to look at me.

There is going to be a typhoon, I said. Maybe tomorrow. They didn't talk about it on the radio this morning, but.

The room looked like a monastic cell. Gloria had her books, textbooks for Cantonese, Pekinese, Hokkien, dictionaries she no longer consulted, except very rarely. She didn't even pretend to throw herself into this impossible task of learning anymore. She no longer had the desire nor the hope of really communicating with anyone.

Do you want to go down into the courtyard, I proposed.

I softly caressed her brows, her cheeks.

She didn't react.

Did you write down any new slogans? I asked.

I left my chair and went to read the lines she had traced on a sheet of stationery, in front of the dictionaries. Gathering the watchwords of an unknown war had been, for weeks, the only intellectual activity in which she voluntarily engaged. A civil war ravaged one of the parallel universes where she prowled. I studied the clamors she had heard, the sentences that. Their poetry did not mask the savagery that inspired them, the intolerance, and the will to abominably murder the adversary. During her inner travels, she picked up these commands of assassination and death, and, upon her return, she put them down on the paper, with a felt-tipped pen.

The end of the world for Gloria is bleak, all inextricable ethnic cleansing and extermination species by species, race after race. The ideologies justifying the dark war are totally opaque. There is no ideology in the background of the combats only inhabited by a universal refusal to live.

PIRATES OF THE SECOND SEA, REGROUP!

OFFICERS OF WAXEN SHORES, REGROUP!

CHILDREN OF THE INNER HARBOUR, REGROUP!

FOR ONE BESIEGED CITY, ONE THOUSAND SAILORS WITH GAPING MAWS!

SURVIVORS OF ANTHILL 304, REGROUP!

FOR ONE INJURED CHRYSALID, THREE

That one isn't finished, I said.

The air conditioner switched off. Suddenly you could hear the noises from outside, the regular whimpering of one lunatic in the courtyard, the hammering of the piston throwing itself onto the piles to plant them in the ground, banging and banging with no respite.

Gloria whispered something, but, when I begged her to repeat what she had wanted to tell me, she dug in her heels and kept her mouth closed.

Gloria, I said, little sister.

I examined her in profile, with a tenderness poisoned by pain. She had remained very appealing, despite the lines madness had begun to etch on her face. A white light came through the window and made her gaze shine. You could see that there were velvety brown lighter rays in the black of her iris. She was wearing a Chinese blouse that she was swimming in, trousers made of cheap cloth.

Whether I wanted to or not, I continued to love this woman who was no longer a lover, who had never been an accomplice of my adolescence, a loving sister with whom I could associate countless memories of my youth, nor a companion with whom I would have traversed the long years of disappointment of adulthood. I had met her recently, and in a kind of suicidal conflagration we had made everything disappear that had, millimeter by millimeter, built a past on which to fall back just in case, and, instead of beginning a new life, we had blithely opened the door leading to our death. With a sleepwalker's carelessness we had burst through that door, and, from the very beginning, we had lost our balance, hand in hand we had wandered toward misfortune, each of us dragging the other toward their own version of nothingness, while the fabric of our consciousness was falling apart.

I was responsible for Gloria, I stared at her in silence, I didn't regret finding myself with her at the end of the world, to protect her and to fade away with her until the end. I felt myself passionately chained to this woman.

Now she was silent, foreign, and fragile.

I went to see an opera, I said after a moment.

The air conditioner turned on again.

Meeting at the Fishers' Pavilion, I said.

Ah, she said. The fishers' pavilion.

Yes, I said. Do you want me to tell you about it?

No, she said.

She didn't speak again for two hours. We took a stroll in the courtyard, we walked under the trees, between the senile patients' buildings, we sat on a cement bench, then we came back to be in the cool air.

The sky was at once cloudless and colorless.

I don't know if I will be able to come back tomorrow, I said. Look at the sky. The typhoon looks like it's going to. I will maybe have to stay in Macau for a day or two.

Ah, she said.

I copied down the slogans from the last war, the dark one.

For the injured chrysalid, I said. It's missing half of.

FOR ONE INJURED CHRYSALID, said Gloria, **THREE CARGOS SET ON FIRE ON THE HIGH SEAS!**

I kissed Gloria on the forehead, I left the room, I left the asylum behind me, I got onto a 33, a bus on its way to the city.

The 33 was packed and, starting at the bridge's entrance, it was stuck in traffic. At a snail's pace we crossed the waters that the gusts of wind now made choppy. When I say us, I'm thinking of the passengers pressed one against the others, the students in their white shirts, workers, intransigent and beautiful ageless women who did not look at me, who had passed the age of twenty-five, and would grow no older, at least until the next millennium.

Then I was near my shack again, on the quay, in the heat and fumes. I loitered for a quarter hour under the filthy arcades. I wanted to go home and drift off.

I inhaled a bowl of noodles in a tavern, sucking the four shards of duck bone on the top that smelled like iodine dye, then I stood up.

A few more details for Kotter, I thought.

Breughel was now nearing abasement.

On the edge of the Inner Harbour, the warehouses and the unloading piers have numbers and names.

TAI SING deck, number 27.

CHUN LEI deck, number 29.

HIP LEI deck, number 30.

I HENG deck, number 31.

Between the piles of concrete boats are moored dwarf junks, which bad luck, along with who knows what nautical maladies, seem to have cracked and faded forever.

In the basins, nothing is moving. The water's surface disappears for several meters, swallowed up under cannibalistic vegetation, horrible to see. Climbing stems and leaves are of the most solid kind. They hideously imprison bottles, cardboard packaging, oil barrels, rotten planks, durian peel, pieces of polyethylene, banana and mango skins, dead fish, fishing net floats, jerrycans, poultry bones, Coca-Cola cans, scraps of polyester, remains of food, foul-smelling foams, San Miguel beer cans, papaya juice cans.

Breughel props his elbows on the parapet separating two gray structures.

He lists the trash floating among the plants, he sorts them into categories, so that maybe one day he can recite a list of detritus for Kotter, if Kotter invites him to chat about this or that, about his autobiography or something else.

Breaths of wind make the laundry drying on a junk flap.

Breughel meditates a little, and then he decides finally to head toward Tarrafeiro Alley.

The wind chases clouds of crackling dust in front of him.

He takes Paço de Arcos Street, then walks up Tarrafeiro Street. He circumvents a trash can and disappears between two walls. That's where he lives, in this dark, narrow gully.

Mrs. Fong is sitting on a little bench, near the fish head, which has evolved since the morning. She is listening to the radio broadcasting *The Immortal's Wedding*, or *The White Snake*, or *The Phoenix's Betrothal*.

The operas are innumerable and you get them mixed up, but, beyond the feeling of failure Breughel experiences when he guesses the wrong title, when he doesn't manage to name the work or the artists, who cares?

Breughel turns the key in the lock of his door with difficulty, you would think it had rusted in a few hours, that something inside it is broken, but he isn't worrying about it, he's trying to recognize the distinguishing musical elements, the proper names sighed out by the singer. He doesn't recognize anything. He opens the door.

He enters, and a powerful hand seizes his collar and sends him to the ground with a brutality beyond what. He pivots, dazed, and receives a blow on the jaw.

The room is very dark. You can't see anything. His adversary smells like aftershave.

Is that you, Kotter? sniffles Breughel.

Don't make any noise, recommends Kotter. Above all don't start howling.

I knew you would come, says Breughel.

Don't make any noise, or I'll bleed you dry, recommends Kotter.

MONOLOGUE

All afternoon I had waited for Breughel's arrival, cloistered in the hot and stinking half-light and jumping every time one of the old women in the alley opened her door, each time the noises were so close, the creaking was such that it seemed to me that someone was putting a key into the shack's lock, this rustic fastener that I had had no trouble breaking and then putting back in order, then relocking it from the inside with an improvised skeleton key, and all afternoon, like this, my ear on alert and my organism as if anaesthetized by the dampness and travel fatigue, I searched methodically, turning over first the lower then the upper layers of the Breughelian dump and discovering nothing really informative, because I don't call informative the numerous cockroaches lying dead, poisoned, in a great variety of hiding places, and I don't call instructive either the pistol that is maybe Chinese, maybe Belgian, or perhaps Vietnamese, which I found under the mattress, nor the shoebox where, in a pile, in undated envelopes, lay undated photographs showing temples and monuments and Asiatic streets, among which, from time to time, you suddenly saw the smiling face of Gloria Vancouver, and, as the hours passed, I had allowed to grow in me the certainty that Breughel would bring almost immediately an answer to all my questions, I had irrationally convinced myself that everything would go quickly and painlessly, so that when Breughel, after this long, long wait, was finally in front of me, tied by the neck to the back of the chair on which I had asked him to take a seat, I felt at first disappointed by his poor grace and lies and, as he carried on, on his chair, in a nonconstructive way, I didn't hesitate to hit him again on the solar plexus, all while resuming our conversation where it had gotten bogged down, saying to Breughel Since you have started talking about Gloria Vancouver, continue, I'm listening, then, as Breughel repeated Gloria Vancouver died two years ago, I said You don't really expect me to believe a fib like that, then I ran my hand over my eyes and eyebrows, trying to wipe away part of the sweat and fatigue that were blinding me, and I said again You won't fool me with your morbid tales, Breughel, and I shrugged my shoulders, adding It will take a lot for me to let myself be convinced, and Breughel in turn passed the palm of his hand over his eyes, rubbing the left cavity under his brow bone, then the right, and after about twelve seconds of silence, without hesitation he declared We took a trip to Korea two years ago and she didn't come back, she was run over by a truck in a Seoul street, then he said I don't know what, then he continued, with a kind of tearless sob I don't know how long they keep unclaimed bodies there, then he said Of course I didn't go to the morgue, it would have called the police's attention to the foreign woman's false papers and my own, and, as I encouraged him with a movement, he began to lay out sentences that made up a fairly coherent story, with pauses and silences I left alone because they didn't last long, speaking in a worn-out voice, rather more like a whisper, vibrating with passion, as if my presence allowed him to free himself of a secret too heavy, too long ruminated on between these four walls, black with mildew, in front of these t-shirts in mourning, in the middle of these piles of *South China Morning Post* and these cartons of random papers and these dead or alive cockroaches, saying I don't intend to tell you the details of my relationship with Gloria Vancouver, far from it, then murmuring You should know that they weren't idyllic, however, far from it, then murmuring even more softly Not idyllic, oh, no, then fell quiet, then letting out reticently Those were terrible years, on the contrary, the most stressful and difficult of my existence, the most destructive from any point of view, then, as if this confession of disaster had relieved him, in a more assured voice he said From the first week I regretted this venture, this break with the normal world I was making in the company of a psychotic, but going back was already unthinkable, because Paradise couldn't pardon us, and, as I agreed with a nod of my head, he continued, Going back to Europe would have been walking out in front of death, the horrible death that Paradise knows how to inflict on its traitors, then he said And, at that time, I wasn't ready to, then he continued, I could have abandoned Gloria, because Machado was with her, he would have taken care of her, then he was quiet, and after a sigh, he explained Really she had phases, cycles of great normality, but then she, then he sighed again and he said After two or three months, I had resigned myself, I accepted what fate had in store for me, then he said in a pensive tone Over there where you're from, Kotter, I could have deteriorated more peacefully, then I gave up on a slow extinction over the course of twenty or thirty years, and he went on I chose speed, then he moved in his chair, saying At the beginning, it's true, an extraordinary exaltation comforted me, then I was very much in love, anyway, you have to understand, and Gloria offered me, in spite of everything, a whirlwind that seemed like eternity, and as I encouraged him to continue, he said, a whirlwind of intense physical love, then When you are in your fifties, you're even more sensitive than before to the intoxications of the body, then You know, Kotter, it's an age where sexual fulfillment and romance seem excluded from all probability, then An age where the verdicts have been pronounced and where you are already covered by the dust of death, whatever you might say to comfort yourself or to put up a good front, then he paused, trying to get his hand between the cord and his trachea, complaining that he couldn't breathe, and, as I didn't intervene to untie him, he subsided and said There was that, that late-in-life madness, but there was also that other thing that dazed me and filled me with enthusiasm, then Something magical, and then he explained For the first time in my life, I found myself caught up in an adventure that required of me the same qualities that my characters had to display in my novels, then, after an evasive gesture, he made a short list of these qualities, the desire to leave the real world, lack of interest in the consequences of his actions, an attraction for irreversible actions, a feeling of present disaster, etc., then he swallowed his saliva and said And so, there you have it, I was holding in my arms a very beautiful and very mysterious young woman, a young warrior like the oh so many I had invented, from the most hermetic spheres of the Party, the least known, then, I don't know if you realize, Kotter, a massively attractive girl had fallen in love with me and wasn't faking it, you don't turn away from such a miracle, even if everything indicates from the very beginning that you're committing suicide, then She was lost in her imaginary worlds of secrets and radical crimes, exactly like the heroines I had, then, as I pointed out to him that the comparison between Gloria Vancouver and his female characters didn't need to be repeated *ad infinitum*, he got a dreamy expression and a whimper of nostalgia and he said I was drunk on this during the decisive weeks, then I regretted it but, now, I don't regret it, then We fled, with the help of Machado the Brazilian, we left the official world behind us, the world of the Party, of Paradise, and he protested again about the cord strangling him, but, as I didn't move, he said I know you also came to get that money back, at least what's left of it, then I'll write you a check in a bit, Kotter, before you execute me, since I suppose you are going to execute me, then, as I didn't answer, he assured me that the available sum was still substantial, even though they had begun to spend it, saying I've managed it economically, Kotter, I've never had expensive tastes and, after Gloria died, I reduced my budget to what was strictly necessary to rot here, without any luxuries, then he returned to the main theme of his narration, saying At first this strange woman was capable of acting, and she acted with lucidity and intelligence, and I attributed her great irritability to the fact that our age difference bothered her, then to our difference in status within the Party, because I had only been a fellow traveler, while she played a major role inside secret organs of which she never spoke and for whom fellow travelers must be contemptible individuals, but then I changed my judgment of it, because these periods of extreme irritability that had interrupted our honeymoon phase were soon transformed into hallucinatory crises and depression, horrible depressive periods, then he was quiet, a long time, one minute, two minutes, and I said not a word, because you have to know how not to interrupt a confession, we also learn that in the Party's training centers, he began again It was clear to me very soon that I wouldn't leave her, not because her undeniable charm or her sexual ferocity or the poetry of her madness bound me to her, but also because she had a fragility, the fragility of a child who.

Again, he was quiet.

We listened to the noise of Tarrafeiro Alley. The wind had picked up in the last hour, hour and a half, and it was howling underneath the door. Opera music also wandered about on the other side of the threshold, cymbal clashes structuring the soprano's long solos, melodies where the orchestra played in unison and where everything seemed harsh, the tone of the clarinet, that of the violins, the flute's song. To all this suddenly were added revolting wafts of grilling fish. The music became harsher still, the smell grew thicker.

After this meditative interval he began speaking again, saying Machado made me swear not to abandon her, but it was a superfluous oath, I had known for a long time that I would be responsible for her day and night until one of us was dead, and he added Those years were just a series of grueling alarms and worries, because Gloria's incoherence endangered, every day, the system of middle-class respectability that Machado had set up for us, then A succession of shadows, then Darkening shadows, less and less poetic, then he bowed his head.

He bowed his head as much as the cord cutting into the cartilage of his throat would allow, and that was all. We could hear the scraping of a broom pushing garbage between the alley's puddles, then the Chinese opera, the wind. I waited, then I approached him, and reminded him that I was there and that his conjugal complaints were of less value for me than what I had demanded at the beginning of our interview, concrete information, precise addresses, dates. After several moaning pants, he got back a bit of hoarse voice and said In Seoul, eighteen months and a bit ago, a woman with no papers, a non-Korean, was laid in a drawer of the morgue and, lacking identification, she was numbered, and she began to wait, and in the administrative services around her they began to wait, then they forgot, then This wait won't end, Kotter, whatever you may try to do now, and as, after having asserted that, he remained slumped on his chair, I let a moment go by and got up, wiping away the sweat stinging my eyes, and I went to shuffle through the stack of papers piled near the typewriter, looking for something that could have given new energy to the conversation, and I immediately came across a sentence where my name appeared, and I read The hot air smelled like caged animal and semi-human, sesame oil, grilled fish cheeks, and Kotter was choking on large drops of sweat, and I turned toward Breughel and said You have a literary way of existing within your own existence, Breughel and, as he didn't answer, I said It's disagreeable for people trying to talk to you, and, while at the same time pulling on the cord to continue our dialogue, I repeated Very, very disagreeable, to a point that you don't.

FICTION

A little while later, I walked to the other side of Breughel's monastic bed and went to isolate myself for a minute in the corner arranged for evacuations, fecal or otherwise, a spot in fact less unclean than the bedroom, as Breughel had had the fortitude to attack the problem and cobble together what was needed, then I untied Breughel and allowed him to follow suit, which he did without complaining, disappearing behind the screen for a reasonable time and then docilely coming back to sit down and as, in the nearby house, the one next door or that of the old woman who had spent the afternoon messing around with metal objects, the falsettos of a Chinese lyric duo tacked and drifted, each quatrain crowned with a clash of brass, and as we were there, silent, listening intensely, made dumb by the heat, trying to breathe in unison with the singers, Breughel spoke of the Chinese theater he had had the opportunity to attend in Gloria Vancouver's company, he described the vast bamboo structures built in front of temples, the altar placed across from the stage, behind the spectators, where the deities in whose honor the show was intended sat enthroned, and he now quoted two or three titles, *The Women-Generals of the Family Yang*, *Springtime in the Waterlily Palace*, then he brought up the audience, the retirees and pious people who hummed the melodies along with the artists, but who showed neither admiration nor emotion and didn't applaud when the last note was emitted, immediately leaving the hall, without a glance for the sumptuous figures who—on the boards now once again trivial—held bouquets and waved, and he assured me that nonetheless Guangdong opera was the dominant popular music here, music that the population enjoys day and night, saying You only have to walk five minutes in the old quarter to be convinced, continuing Suddenly the flood of Cantopop dries up, the Anglo-American sound seems out of place, and I'm not about to complain about it, then he invited me to enjoy what was coming from the neighboring house, and which seemed fairly unenjoyable, I'll admit, then he asked me for my opinion of the qualities of the singer and, in reaction to my noncommittal response, he screwed up his mouth and shrugged his shoulders, then was quiet.

A little later still, as I returned to the question of Gloria Vancouver's accidental demise in Korea, Breughel went to find an envelope in a cardboard box I had recently searched, and then, while I rid myself of the briny humors pearling in front of my eyes, he showed me tourist brochures about Seoul, then a first photograph of Gloria Vancouver, all the documents I had scanned during my inspection and that hadn't seemed worthy of any particular attention, and on the back of the snapshot he read a caption written in pencil, saying It was taken in front of Kyongbok, and, as I could no longer make anything out in the shadows, I went to flip the switch near the door and the bulb lighted up, illuminating the room as only sixty watts can, smearing with a sinister glare this space whose once-white, or at least pale, ambiance had suffered the outrages of tropical humidity and miasmas, with its furniture that looked exactly like the furniture of temporary lodgings during an eviction and which was crumbling under the chaos and artificial shadows, then I sat back down so I could examine what he wanted me to examine, other photos of Gloria Vancouver that he now held out to me, each time squinting at the information scrawled on the back, then announcing the name of the place with phonetic exoticisms that annoyed me, saying now An afternoon at Toksu palace, sometimes That day we went to see the Namhansansong fortress, sometimes the Chongryangri, one morning, or abbreviating his commentary even further, reducing it to a curselike sound, Taenung, Pukansansong, Kumgoknung, or Namdaemun, Tongdeamun, and, as I had set down on the bed in front of me the young woman's portraits, attributing no importance to the urban landscapes, nor to the tombs, nor to the interweaving of superb roofs and walls, preferring to examine the ravaged face of Gloria Vancouver, the shape of her smile altered by her mental tempests, her gaze where a slow nightmare was being distilled in darkness and flames, as I didn't speak, he said From far away, I saw the accident, it was late in the morning, on Chongno, on Chongno Avenue, then he murmured We had argued, and he murmured again We argued about everything, then She always found something to complain about, to accuse me of, and he added It was terrifying, and, in a scarcely audible tone, he repeated For me, life had transformed into a wandering, devoid of interest and terrifying, and he whispered again I couldn't take it anymore, then he said, but in a less distorted voice, now firmer, From far away I saw a man in a lab coat hide her face with a sheet, and he coughed and said When a doctor covers someone up like that in the middle of the road, the diagnosis has no ambiguity, and he paused, then he got up and drank a glass of water from the tap, then he came back to slouch on the chair, saying You know, Kotter, sometimes we can act strangely, then I found myself at a certain distance, one hundred meters, two hundred meters, often more, because I never approached the troupe, I only circled around the immense intersection where the accident had taken place, freezing at various spots on the edge of the sidewalk to observe the crowd, the ambulance, the police immobile near a newspaper kiosk, then next to a tree, then in front of the door of a fast food restaurant, and this attitude, in the morning, seemed to me to be the only one possible, and he said again I considered all of this with glacial objectivity, I felt no emotion, no confusion, and You know, Kotter, each of us harbors a monster, an occasion like this is enough to realize it, then he launched into a description of the shock and the trajectory that Gloria, after having been thrown in front of the wheels, followed over the top of the pickup truck, saying things like I saw her, spinning to the side, or She fell upright onto the asphalt with an acrobat's suppleness, or It seemed that her hair was suddenly very long and very shiny, and she softly shook that black mane in theatrical fashion, hiding inside herself, no longer wishing anything but to look like a dancer, or She took two steps to the left, she staggered but seemed to be alright, then she lay down softly, beneath her hair, while the pickup truck finished braking, and then he panted for a minute, letting the drops of sweat drip down all over his cheeks, then he launched himself into his tale again without me having to push him around, beginning to stir again and obstinately give shape to the basic elements.

    In the alley, dusk had ceded place to night, and the wind was blowing stronger and stronger. Endless gravel was thrown against the door, clods of dirt. The piles of newspapers pulsed under the table, near the bed. I felt the hot breath around my legs. I was sweating. I was hungry, the jet lag made my mind waver. Breughel was talking.

    He lifted his eyes toward the mildew that formed a velvety layer on the ceiling, and at first he said It's useless to try to recreate it for you, Kotter, the imbecilic discussion we had had that morning, it contained the same amount of abjection and madness as those that went before, and then he said In short, Gloria had left the room without the least identification, then he began to think out loud about what the Seoul police must have tried to identify the foreign woman, saying The boss of the *yogwan* where we had a room was not interested in our civil status, he took us for two English tourists, and added The only document that contained a trace of her passage was the disembarkation file at the airport, a tiny piece of paper lost in an immense mess, then saying A slim trail for the investigators, then immediately correcting himself, Besides, the police weren't going to send their best teams to clear up the ins and outs of a traffic accident, it wasn't a criminal affair after all, and, as I didn't interrupt him, he continued to speculate on that theme, then he came back to the scene in the street and he said I was paralyzed, then I saw the sheet cover Gloria completely, and my first reflex was to think that this death was my salvation, luck to be seized upon, in any case, and then I was ashamed, then he remained speechless for a few seconds, then he said You don't know, Kotter, what it is to share your daily life with a psychotic, what hell that is like, then he said There is no surrealist beauty in madness, then Every moment, she covered her anxiety with bitter rage, about everything, then he repeated Bitter rage, a constant state of irrational suffering, then he murmured The devouring selfishness of the mad, and he went on She tried to drag me down into her illogical abyss, she always wanted to convince me and, seeing me resist, the rage would take over, then he sighed and said You can't understand, Kotter, what, then he said When you resist day after day, for months, years, when on top of that you live a hunted life in a distorted truth, then he said You feel an underground gnawing by a tireless fear, you know that anything ugly and stupid might happen, and shrunk down into himself and whispered Tomorrow is uncertain, the next hour is uncertain, then he was quiet, while the wind whistled on the other side of the door, then he said And the hate, Kotter, the hate that accumulates, criminal hopes that grow and haunt you, and I counted nine seconds of silence, and after a mournful, startled gesture he added In the end she had to have someone who stayed at her side to keep her from too irreparably lacerating the epidermis of the reality where she had taken refuge, to protect her from what might come, from Paradise, and he said again At all costs I had to keep helping her, but his voice was cracking more and more and he cleared his throat and added There was no longer any poetry or love between us, Kotter, just that, the painful sense of obligation.

Breughel had closed his eyes. I had untied him a short while ago so he could go urinate, and, after that episode, I hadn't bound his legs or neck to the chair again. He was resigned to my presence. I dominated him physically and he knew that any attempt at resistance or flight would be met with reprisals. He was sitting nearly still, within slapping range. From time to time I would wave my fake M39 Smith & Wesson in front of his face and I would hit him on the cheekbones with the butt, but, most often, he was talking spontaneously. I had wrapped the pistol I had found between the mattress and the bed frame in newspaper and put it in one of my jacket pockets, the left, I think, I didn't see its use for me.

Chased away by the wind, the old women of the alley had left their dark doorways and retired into greater darkness in their dens where the only lighted lamp was the one glowing red behind a statuette, above an offering as humble as it was miserly, a slice of orange, a dumpling, a cookie, and, sheltered, they continued their ruminations, listening to *Dream in the Ant Kingdom*, *Long Visits His Mother*, or *Lam Chong Flees in the Night*. A new excerpt of Guangdong opera rang out, as it happened, arranged around a male monologue, plaintive, monotonous, and opaque. The noise of the wind distorted it, but you could hear.

Breughel was still breathing. His eyes were closed and his eyelids continuously fluttered.

I began to observe Breughel's worn-out features and I superimposed onto them those of the sick woman whose photos were lined up in front of me, on the bed, like the cards of a game of solitaire, doing my best to revive mentally the Breughel-Vancouver couple, trying to represent mentally for myself this union, revealing these two beings in the light of what Breughel had confided in me and seeing in it, in spite of it all, poetry and love, then Breughel opened his eyes and said I acted like a killer, like I guess killers must act, with their dirty souls bothered by nothing, then he said I went back to the *yogwan* where we had a room, I gathered up all her things in my bag, then, I left, and then he said Once set up in a new room in a different neighborhood, I destroyed her passport, her papers, her plane ticket, then he speculated again about the border control's computer programs, getting lost in his rationalizing and reaching no conclusion, then he returned to his tale and said The next day I got to the airport early, then he wiped the front of his t-shirt with palms wet from anxiety, and, after avoiding my gaze, he said, My heart drained, I got through all the departure formalities, fearing every second that someone would interrogate me as to why Gloria wasn't with me at registration, but, as our tickets had been booked separately, no one of course thought to associate our names, then he remained for a moment lost under the influence of this memory, and, for a moment, nothing was exchanged between us, and I took advantage of this to follow along with an orchestral phrase of *Dream in the Ant Kingdom*, then Breughel revived and went to rummage around beside his typewriter, and after having explored several piles of papers, he held out to me a new photo of Gloria Vancouver, on the back of which I deciphered, half out loud, *Insadong, Chongno,* larvae, and, as I demanded an explanation with furrowed brows, even a succinct one, he said Insadong is a neighborhood, Chongno is an avenue, it's in downtown Seoul, five hundred meters from the *yogwan* where we were staying, and he added In the streets they sell boiled silkworm chrysalids, cooked or reheated in a brown sauce, then he said the seller gives you a ladleful in a disposable cup, then he said Gloria liked that kind of thing, not the food itself, but the idea, the strange experience, and I nodded circumspectly while looking at the last picture of the young woman, a little different from the others in the sense that you could see in Gloria Vancouver's smile, beyond her ordinary distress, a gourmet's excitement, a childlike passion that must certainly have had some fleeting relationship with happiness, then Breughel said For my part, I don't much enjoy eating dead animals, then he let half a minute go by and added, I enjoy it less and less, and he insisted, saying When I eat meat, I have to force myself to forget that it's meat, then he cleared his throat and snapped at me I don't know what it's like for you, Kotter, but I have a tendency to believe that a killer must not ask himself that kind of question much, then, as I didn't answer, just spreading out, on the pillow, on the sheets, the many photos of Gloria Vancouver, and, reflecting, turning around from every angle this Seoul story without finding one crack or incoherence, Breughel put out his hand toward the snapshot titled *Insadong, Chongno,* larvae, and he took it back and looked at it without noticeable emotion and while, behind the wall, the two-string violins and wooden drums accompanied the sinuous declamation of a singer, her incomprehensible wail, he was quiet, then he said In the streets there are kettles where the chrysalids simmer, and from these escapes a smell that can't be compared to anything else, and, as I raised my head in his direction The taste is rather dull, then he said At any rate you know what you're biting into, you know exactly what you're taking apart with your tongue, and you'd rather think that the taste reminds you of dust rather than insects, slightly salted sawdust, and our gazes met again and he said On the other hand, the smell is strong, it lingers around the stalls on the sidewalk, it's a smell that I would recognize among a thousand others, and he added I still have it in my nose, then he had a nervous spasm that he overcame and he said I find it again in my mind every time I think of Seoul, then he corrected himself and he said Every time I think of Gloria Vancouver's death in Seoul.

FICTION

I

Kotter closed the refrigerator door. He seemed disappointed. The device functioned and managed to delay with some success the putrefaction of some bits of leftover food, but as for refreshments, nothing, two cartons of soy milk occupied the compartment reserved for bottles. And certainly the idea would never occur to Kotter to taste a beverage made from pressing beans and their sprouts.

The water, can I, he asked.

What, said Breughel.

The tap water, said Kotter. Can you drink it without risk of.

He recalled his research on Southeast Asia. In general, you could, but, out of prudence, it was better to stick to ingesting boiled water, distributed in hotels by porters.

Without risk of what, said Breughel.

Kotter sputtered out the beginning of a word, then turned on the tap and splashed his face. He avoided taking in the smallest drop, so as not to be contaminated by the hepatitis virus or one of the numerous bacteria active in the humid tropical zone, he carefully spat out the tepid trickle that had made its way into his mouth.

Now he bent down to explore the cupboard. The unit held up the sink and served as a towel holder for the two gingham dishrags on which Breughel wiped his hands. The pattern didn't look unclean but gave off a foul smell. A handful of poisonous grains languished near a pipe, promising tetanus and narcosis to the hungry shadows, promising them fuchsia pink suffering, Tyrian pink and primrose convulsions.

Despite the poison, however, life went on.

A column of Lilliputian ants advanced toward a bottle of gas.

Farther on, under the rusted base of the refrigerator, a roach with a passion for exercise was making scissoring motions with its antennae.

Kotter was rummaging through the stock of food cartons, quarter-liters full of chrysanthemum tea. A transparent straw was glued to each yellowish box.

You might have put them in the fridge, said Kotter.

Oh I don't know about that, said Breughel.

The straw being cut at an angle, Kotter stabbed it through the container's mouth, then sucked on it. After a few seconds, the sucking noise got louder. The carton was visibly collapsing. Already you could track the last sips, their taste of paper and slimy paraffin.

Kotter, thinking of nothing in particular, played with the wet noises of the empty carton. He thus called up in Breughel some banal childhood memories, drinking with a straw, traces of *diabolo menthe* under an ice cube that hadn't entirely melted. All of a sudden I thought of vacations in summer, the hubbub of a conversation among grownups. Some adults laughed carelessly, others were watching the sparkling, quiet waves. The little ones blew bubbles, exchanging untranslatable bubble speeches.

Kotter finished smashing the carton he was holding near his lips, then he threw it into the supermarket bag, which, under Breughel's worktable, gaped open to receive nonperishable trash that could be smashed up and which the vermin ignored. Mechanically, on the colored side of the bag, the Party's killer observed the characters he couldn't read. An address was there, printed in two languages. A series of magnificent characters, then **OCEAN GARDEN, PEACH COURT, TAIPA**.

The carton of tea began to uncrumple with a furtive crackling. It had landed on a plastic pouch that now Kotter was observing impassively, although something dangerous had awoken in the shadows of his brain a line of reasoning that hadn't yet found a conscious formulation. Again, the killer scanned the beautiful characters. Landscape writing, a caress for the eye. Then the English translation New Century Hotel, Cakeshop, Taipa. Taipa.

Ah, he said.

He turned toward Breughel with an almost benevolent expression.

Now, behind the mask, his brain had just. Association had just been born.

Breughel was slumped on the chair. He turned an exhausted eye toward the photographs spread out in front of him, news of Seoul, Insadong, Chongno, which are, let's recall, a capital, a downtown neighborhood, an avenue.

What Breughel was seeing and reliving remained an enigma. He seemed absorbed in the evocation of a past inside which you couldn't guess where he situated himself, nearby or in the distance. The shiny film of the paper came between Gloria Vancouver and himself, and across this membrane of death they watched each other, immobile and dreamy. You couldn't say whether they were really separated or moving about inside the same world.

The wind shook the door.

In Tarrafeiro Alley, someone had turned off the radio after it had played *The Companion with the Enchanting Perfume* or *The Swallow's Letter*.

The scene now played out without musical accompaniment, with raw sound effects.

Grainy dust rattled against the outside wall.

A piece of corrugated metal, somewhere, imitated a peal of thunder.

The heat had not abated.

The carton continued to bring its mistreated cellulose back in place, popping and crackling, and as Kotter, with the instinctive curiosity of a predator, went to see if a rodent wasn't by any chance wriggling around in the paper trash, he noticed the wrapper from some ginger candy, made in the **TONG PAK CHONG** pastry shop, Taipa.

Taipa. Around it a hypothesis could take shape.

I wonder, said Kotter.

What? asked Breughel.

Nothing, said Kotter. I was thinking about the wind.

II

Signal 1, a tropical storm is afloat on the China Sea.

Signal 3, it's heading toward the territory.

Signal 8, it's here. Taipa bridge is closed to traffic. The island becomes an island again. Gusts reach one hundred nautical miles per hour. The junks take shelter in flocks in certain illusory spots in the harbor where the wind seemed less ferocious. The sky is opening up onto the world and howling. Rain runs across the city horizontally. Nothing is flowing away anymore, the sewers are overflowing. In the old quarters, the water doesn't stop rising, it carries along tumultuous deposits where gray and black trash jumbles together. The wind tears away fences, signs. Bamboo scaffolding falls apart.

Signal nine, signal ten, the eye of the hurricane is less than one hundred nautical miles from the territory. On top of the old fort, sirens are sounded that no one hears because of the din. The radio broadcasts programs electrified by on-the-ground reporting. The authorities advise pushing heavy furniture against the windows, against the doors. In spite of all this, windows shatter, doors explode.

III

An old woman, in front of the departure deck IAO TAC, number 23, pushes aside the rags she has been dozing under until now. She gets up. The wind is disturbing her, the wind is blowing too hard now.

With decrepit steps, she crosses the road.

The guts of poorly closed or tipped-over containers begin to spread out under the dark arcades of the Inner Harbour, Lorchas Street, Visconde Paço de Arcos Street, Almirante Sergio Street, Ribeira de Patane Street. Detritus spins in the air at head height, at lamppost height, and then it rains down on the stagnant water of the holding basins, it drums down on the leaves of the ugly aquatic plants growing there, on the roofs of the sampans, on the boats.

Above the Inner Harbour, the moon has ended its brief flirtations. In the gaps in the clouds, it underlined the ragged speed at which the vapor was contorting itself, then it disappeared, although not without some hide-and-seek. But then the sky tarred up all its cracks.

The city is dreaming loudly.

The wind is howling.

In the run-down neighborhoods, it shakes the thousands and thousands of padlocked iron shutters, the cages sticking out of the front of the apartment buildings, the incalculable number of grates protecting Chinese households from thieves and murderers, then, underneath the arcades, it pummels the metal shutters fending off burglars, their accordion folds, thrashing them ferociously, then it goes to whistle over the boards and sheets of corrugated metal nailed over uninhabitable ground floors, in front of abandoned storefronts, the abandoned stores reeking of musty earth and dead plaster.

An ugly corrugated slab floats for two seconds above the woman in rags, then it rears up, then finishes its flight on the hood of a truck parked across from the disembarkation pontoon number 22A, quite near Tarrafeiro Street. The din is audible inside Breughel's house.

Below the docks, the water is lapping.

The floating casino's lights shine as if nothing were happening.

Lanterns dance on the prows of the junks.

The signs in the whole neighborhood are flapping.

DENTISTA LEUNG YAN SO
FARMACIA CHINESA IAN VO CHEONG KEI
RESTAURANTE MENG WA
ARTIGOS ELECTRICOS VENG HENG
AGENCIA COMERCIAL SAN PUI KEI
GARAGEM WONG KEI
DR. SUN SAI YING, MÉDICO

On their hinges, the flea-bitten doors shake.

Into each crevice, the roaring demons blow sawdust.

A song of disintegration buffets the human forms that breathe and pretend not to hear anything.

On the other shore, the People's Republic is very dark.

The beggarwoman leans into the wind, bent over. Her trousers slap against her impossibly thin legs. The fabric of her collarless jacket suddenly shines oddly beneath a streetlight.

Then she disappears.

She's a thousand-year-old woman. She's going to take shelter.

She has an extraordinarily photogenic face, the face of the earth itself, and on the corner of Tarrafeiro Street she belches, then she disappears.

IV

What about the wind, asked Breughel.

You think we're going to have a typhoon? said Kotter.

I don't know, said Breughel. Maybe just a tropical storm. Severe or not. There's a whole system of nomenclature for.

Kotter scowled. He wasn't thinking about questions of meteorological vocabulary.

There was a silence.

When are you going to execute me? asked Breughel.

Kotter walked to and fro inside the room. He bent down to pick up notebooks, sketch pads, bundles of papers that he skimmed quickly and which always spoke of the same thing, the sordid scenery, night noises, heat, Guangdong opera, inaccessible Chinese women, Gloria's death, Gloria's mental breakdown, and also Breughel's miserly monasticism, this quest for degradation that Breughel was accomplishing here, foreign to everything, instead of going back to

Europe to die in his own culture and language. A choice that could only be explained by a pathological tendency to self-hatred and suicide.

Or by the fact that Breughel maintained ties to Macau, sentimental and physical.

Among the writings that caught Kotter's attention there were lists and slogans whose origins and motives weren't

CHRYSALIDS OF THE THIRD SLEEP, REGROUP!

YOUR LIFE SAVED, SOLDIER, IF YOU DENOUNCE A DESERTER!

FOR ONE PIRATE SUBJECTED TO TORTURE, ONE VILLAGE VITRIFIED!

INCENDIARIES OF THE SAFFRON MOONS, REGROUP!

CHILD OF THE EIGHTH ARMY, HANG YOURSELF WITH YOUR BELT!

INCENDIARY OF THE SAFFRON MOONS, HANG YOURSELF WITH YOUR BELT!

Kotter, wordlessly, scanned these barbaric ruins of grandiloquence. Faith in the future had arrived there at the final degree of its suicidal combustion.

What is this, he finally asked.

This what, said Breughel.

Chrysalids of the ninth banner, pirates of quicksilver seas, cited Kotter.

He referred to a list he was holding. They all looked alike. They were numerous.

Ah, yes, said Breughel.

What is it, said Kotter.

As Breughel was maneuvering so as not to have to answer, Kotter went over and hit him.

It was the signal for the start of a new disorganized scuffle between the bed and the chair, in the middle of the photographs of Gloria Vancouver that had been scattered when he fought back, when he had blocked Kotter's blows and even, out of habit, tried to neutralize and beat Kotter with a jiu-jitsu hold suggested by his memory, a twist of the cubitus followed by a dislocation of the elbow. Kotter had just grimaced, then hit him.

What is it, Kotter asked again.

Sentences of Gloria's, sentences like. Like she would say, stammered Breughel. I elaborated on them. I tried to include them in stories.

I see, said Kotter.

If you want to read one, proposed Breughel, pointing to a cardboard box.

He stayed crouched at the foot of the bed, a little swollen or scraped here and there, short of breath.

Oh, you know, I'm not much of a one for reading, said Kotter.

DREAM

III

The night stretched on eternally. A thousand slouching vagabonds murmur the prayers and moans of half-sleep. And so the hours pass. The maritime station is stuck in a world where even the idea of dawn seems to be banished. Dreams ferment collectively and suddenly, well before morning, a hallucination takes shape, waking the rabble and stirring it up.

Escaped from a suburban menagerie, maddened by freedom, an elephant has entered the lower city. After having run through the streets, trumpeting, it emerges onto the esplanade of the port, and immediately, it rushes toward the barriers blocking access to the sea.

You shouldn't fire at an elephant but, poorly evaluating the nature of the incident, awed, a small soldier set off a hail of bullets onto the tons of flesh trying to force their way through those obstacles. Now the pachyderm is staggering along the barriers. It's angry at the unexpected suffering and at this garland of hot orchids blooming on its abdomen.

The hubbub increases. The elephant hits the barrels full of sand, trips on the movable safety fences. It undoes several coils of wire, continuing for seven or eight meters, then it stops. A corporal runs up to it, his mouth overflowing with obscene curses and accusations, and, as no one comes to back him up, he swallows his rage and falls back to the patrol.

The enormous animal teeters at the edge of the barbed wire, just in front of the gangway to the port, which, for the moment, remains closed. It stamps its feet, trunk lowered, repeatedly trying to start a forward movement, irresistible but stopped short, followed by a recoil, followed immediately by a new unaccomplished impulse toward the front.

It's a morbid dance step.

You dance like that when you know you're going to die.

The excitement has reached the open-air dormitory. In the darkness fights break out. Without establishing any distinction between species, lice change their partners one last time. Ghosts massage their stiffened limbs, and then they go crouch over the garbage piles to defecate. You, little brother, you overcome the malarial torpor and get up. You have to work against your aching muscles. You have to refuse to believe in the vertigo. You zigzag between the gleams of lit cigarettes in this dense population. You have to constantly reconstruct yourself, because the shaking is undoing you. You want to see the elephant, you are thinking about the elephant, but, after a minute: your obsession.

Your obsession takes over again. The islands, flee to the islands, join Gloria. Be allowed on the other side of the military checkpoint.

Leaving. Gloria.

Behind the *chevaux de frise*, soldiers are already regrouping, and some of them are screwing the bayonets that they had taken off for the night back onto their guns, but it's the elephant that moderates the aggressive impulses of the refugees and worries them. In the light of their torches, without trumpeting, not showing its pain, it's in its death throes. It's standing. The wild darkness crushes the stains on the ground. Bits of glass, sand, feathers. You come closer, little brother. Cement, columns of ants, lizards.

You can scarcely see anything. You hear the muscles wracked by spasms. You imagine what is under its hide. Its side has furrows plowed by the fences. In its open wounds bubble viscous streams. You examine the scabs and hairs of the feet miming a walk. You come still closer. Over the top of your natural sympathy for the animal grows a kind of querulous malevolence, because deep down you are afraid that the elephant's presence will keep the soldiers from opening this barrier that represents the border. You question the tiny eye hiding in the giant head and nothing answers you, but you understand that, behind this mass with no gaze, its obstinacy is melting. So only your compassion grows. On top of the gusts of fuel oil and saltwater coming from the harbor, you inhale the animal's anxiety. You receive its messages of supplicant sweat, its breath where saliva laps against death. Now, you too, little brother, the fever has you and ravages you, and that coincidence makes you panic. This similarity. You don't want your two fates to. Drops of sweat roll down your chest, anxiety and malady in one icy thread.

You begin to sway from one foot to the other. You imagine your death in front of the spiky bushes, under the deluge of insults from the corporal. You invent stupid and repugnant variations. Any bad luck could come before dawn. The drops of sweat roll and roll. You shiver.

At that moment, someone touches your arm and speaks to you. Someone has mistaken you for someone else. They're asking you for some information in a dialect spoken by the Westerners in your battalion. You pretend not to understand a single word. You don't look at your interlocutor. You turn away. You make yourself hide your face. Is this man an old comrade from the front? Did he recognize something in your features? And what if, after three seconds of mental confusion, he was going to remember you and, breaking with all logic, cursing the tragedy of your two existences, roust the military police, bellow your name, your number, denounce you as a deserter?

You shrink back, you rejoin the herd circling on the esplanade. The refugees walk in the shadows waiting for daylight. The groups have split up. No one is playing the flute anymore. No one is sitting or lying down anymore. Your heart is a drum without a master. You get the impression that you have just barely escaped something irreparable, only just barely.

You stay near a pile of rubbish for an hour, in the nauseating to-and-fro. The light is very weak, and, on the dirty walls, you read with difficulty the characters of some propaganda.

A DAY OF COMBAT = A CENTURY OF PEACE IN AMBER!

AN AUTUMN OF COMBAT = A THOUSAND YEARS OF PEACE IN AMBER!

DESERTER OF THE EASTERN FRONT, HANG YOURSELF WITH YOUR BELT!

IV

And then the melee starts, the shock of grinding bone on muscles, the kicks, your bleeding side, the unconscious wounded who don't fall. The soldiers come to open up the chokepoint through which the candidates for departure are supposed to file—one by one. An everyman-for-himself increases the violence, the selfishness. You aren't any different from the others, little brother. You go forward, you blaze a trail, and not one of your movements isn't inspired in equal parts by stupidity and murderous slyness.

And now you have to walk by this dying animal. The soldiers were too stingy in pushing apart the *chevaux de frise*. The crowd continues to fear the sudden madness of the pachyderm and fights at the same time to get into the border bottleneck and not to brush up too closely to the monster panting at the entrance to the barrier. Sometimes the trunk springs to life, taking out one or two travelers. A man knocks against you. Your trousers are caught, tear, you pull on the cloth, you get away. Legs bent, off balance, you throw the man into the roll of barbs, and here you are feeling up against you that hot wall shaking and stinking. You contort yourself to regain your balance. You touch the velvety bumps of the immense skull. The ear immediately convulses around you, an immense manta ray. Finally it's your turn. A metal screen already separates you from the esplanade. You've rejoined the line progressing slowly toward the checkpoint. You've passed.

Barbed wire, a jeep, a truck. Eight soldiers commanded by a lieutenant of the Armies of the She-Wolf. You're out of breath. You are sweating and your teeth are chattering.

When your turn comes, you hold out a false military enrollment book and your fake visa from High Command XII, and your fake orders for the islands. A torch crackles next to your cheek. There's not a chink in the dark night. You're stuck between the fish traps and the border fence, and here is where everything is decided. Two soldiers pat down your rags, looking for a weapon. The humid heat envelops all of us. The lieutenant perspires in large drops. The bottom of his face had been burned with acid. He weighs your life, examines the signatures, the texts. He looks at your photograph in the light. His fingers are burned too. You, little brother, you are like the elephant, you have trouble accepting the eventuality of death before daybreak. You have bunches of brown orchids in your mind's eye. The soldiers stare at you, in silence. Into the truck parked twenty meters away, they make the conmen climb, or those who try to get a knife, a hook, or some other dangerous object across the border, and they knock them out with shovels. The pile of bodies has already reached proportions that. The lieutenant opens his charcoal mouth and asks your function in the war. You answer that you are an interpreter. He asks you why you don't have any baggage. You state that someone stole your bag. You don't have enough air to breathe. You say it's malaria. Ah, malaria, says the lieutenant. Your eyes see the puddle with no color growing beneath the truck. Oil, maybe. The lieutenant makes a vague gesture. He points to the boat. He gives your papers back to you. He doesn't care about you anymore. The bayonets don't escort you to the truck. On the departure quay a shadow goes ahead of you, fifteen steps ahead, as terrified or stupefied as you are. You thought that. The ordeal seemed interminable to you, but, in reality, it only lasted a few seconds.

You walk toward the gangway piercing the black cliff of the cargo ship. At the end of the quay shimmer a lantern and some stars. Near a hangar an empty bus is parked. The landscape is motionless. Your legs are shaking. Behind you, the border lights illuminate the elephant's death throes. Vehicles and soldiers stay in the shadows. Beyond the loops of barbed wire the refugees are invisible. You can hear the constant murmur of the crowd, but you don't see individuals. In the truck, the queue-jumpers are dying without a cry.

You cross the gangway and, when you put your foot on the bridge, watchwords in Kordve assail you.

LITTLE CHRYSALIDS, REGROUP!

SOLDIERS, SAILORS, NO ALLIANCE WITH CIVILIANS!

SISTERS OF THE SEVENTH SHIPWRECK, REGROUP!

V

The day is breaking, little brother, and you are leaning on the rail of the upper bridge. You've chosen not to look at the sea. You aren't on the side where the harbor opens. You aren't examining the gray water, the submerged fishing boats, scuttled on the harbor master's orders, the dead rowboats and junks. The seas tremble in little waves above the shipwrecks. That's not what you're looking at.

Leaning over the starboard, you tower over the port. The access to the quay has been closed for a quarter of an hour. The crowd's protests haven't ended. The break of dawn was painful to everyone. On the esplanade the living and the dead are laid out pell-mell. Several are lying between the elephant's feet, in the puddle of reddish urine that the animal emitted at the twilight of its existence. Now the pachyderm had lost its great size and nobility. It's no longer trembling and it's going to die. On this side of the barbed wire, the good side, the executed queue jumpers have disappeared. First the truck, then the bus took them away somewhere.

The miracle survivors like you are quiet around you, in their hundreds. Each one is isolated in their rags and their thoughts, little brother, feeling the new sensations of salvation: the metal railing under your arm, the remorse at having survived, the shame of being.

You lean over. A new squadron of military police is taking the gangway. It's High Command XII's order that will rule during the crossing. You haven't seen a single sailor until now. Infantry soldiers are circulating on the boat and taking care of the maneuvers.

At the idea of the crossing, your mind goes back to the themes dear to it. Gloria is there. You wander amongst the trees and she is there. Her long black hair touches your shoulder, she exists next to you, you take her hand, her wrist, she pulls away, she talks to you. She has a voice worn out by absence. Her lips move. She says something about the low branches. The beach sparkles behind the leaves. Again, her hair brushes against you. It is a very precise and very beautiful caress.

It's been a long time since the motor started. Without jolting, the cargo ship leaves the dock. Two soldiers are folding up the collapsible half of the gangway on the bow. Beneath you a triangle of ashen water is spreading out. The droning of the screws vibrates along your bones. The vibration grows. The outlines of faces lose their clarity. The contours become blurred.

At this moment a gaze pierces your back, and you turn around, and you notice, slumped on the duckboard of the bridge and pretending not to see you, the man who had addressed you that night in the crowd. He's wearing a black cap and clothes shiny with motor oil. You might think he was a worker from the arsenal. Now you recognize him. He's a runaway like you, a renegade from the Sixth Battalion of the regular army, a deserter, and you could call the guard and point him out to the guard, and scream and scream his name that all of a sudden comes back to you: Machado.

The screws' movement reverses, the structure vibrates with a metallic noise. You are five steps from this man, this Machado of the Sixth Battalion. And you are trembling.

VI

Soldier, the army offers you its mercy if you.

Your life saved if you give one up.

And what follows, little brother. The ignominy that follows. The military police dragging on the between-decks stairs two demons cursing in spite of the boots kicking their mouths in, both bellowing, each one claiming to have yelled first to denounce the other. You splatter him with bloody phlegm, and you remember Machado your war buddy, a hardened warrior, efficient, taciturn. You often found yourselves in comparable situations, kitted out the same for an assault. You see him again scratching off his uniform the tar from a sticky bomb, then trembling beneath his mask before leaving again in the middle of the cinders. And there you are, foaming at the mouth face to face, beaten and beaten by the soldiers. For an uninformed spectator, it is impossible to say which one betrayed the other, which of the two will rejoin the front and which one will be tortured with monstruous games, slowly, before being thrown to the orcas.

It's hard to tell, but you know it instinctively, little brother. It's you who.

The machines strain away in the depths.

Machado has disappeared.

Land is now nothing but an abstract idea. An arid islet, a last handful of wrecked junks, then a few gulls turning around, then nothing.

You walk to and fro on the boat, hoping to avoid Machado, inside your hallucinations aggravated by awful calculations. You go over and over from the upper bridge to between decks, often crossing paths with the military police. Cowardice trembles beneath your fingernails.

There are no women on board. The war's population is animal or human, but now it only counts among it masculine ruins, former killers, old trench cleaners, criminals in uniform, and traitors.

VII

When the cargo ship is completely immobile, when the second bridge fills with shouts, you are leaning against the guardrail in the shadow of a lifeboat, and you are watching the wake, the marbling in the gray sea doesn't heal. Your hands scrape the scales of rust on the most recent layer of white. You try to decipher the cries, the echoes. An abnormal agitation contorts the ship's insides. You don't move. You don't go ask what's happening. You know that you occupy a strategic space, because of the fresh air, the departure.

Less than a minute later, the stern is filled with people. A heterogeneous mass floods toward you from the gangway. Faces and undone turbans, gazes that meet by accident and turn away, incapable of forming any communication. No one is talking. No soldiers are visible. Around you rises the stench of terror. When nightmares are marinating inside us, it acidifies our flesh and glands.

You defend your spot and lower your eyes along the hull. A vertical ladder leads down toward the screws. The last rungs are lapped by the very calm water. The sun isn't shining anywhere. The weather is hot and overcast. On the sides of the miniscule waves no foam appears. If you had to abandon ship, the ladder wouldn't necessarily be useful. You stare at the dinghy suspended in the sky in front of you, out of reach, hanging by cables and flying buttresses the sailors call davits. The protective tarp makes the lifeboat seem unwelcoming for the moment, but ten or so people could get into it in case of a shipwreck. A reduction system controls its descent to water level. There are two pulleys, one for each davit.

The doors continue to vomit forth a languageless mob, exhausted wrecks whose future and appearance no longer make any sense. They keep their thoughts to themselves and they are content to emerge with a waxy physiognomy where all transparency is peeled away. To know how much the ugliness of the present is affecting them, you would have to be an expert in matters of the soul. You can feel the vibrations breaking apart their thoughts behind the mask, you sniff the odors of bodies in distress, but, on their faces, none of this shows through. You would have to know how to dive in beyond their pupils and that's an old intuitive wisdom that you've forgotten, little brother, that you've lost while wandering the paths of mass murder.

The weight accentuates against your injured side, you shift your weight to one foot like when you used to handle a flamethrower. You meet a few gazes questioningly. You analyze them with hungry impoliteness. In the inky blackness of an iris you sometimes think you catch a masochistic relief, certainty about the end of the voyage, then the communication is muddied. You no longer have the finesse that.

But then you meet Machado's eyes, which have been locked on you for several seconds. Your companion in carnage has made his way off the gangway and he's watching you. There's one whose intimate feelings you understand with no trouble, because you attribute to him all of the conscious or unconscious quagmire that governs you. And you persuade yourself that you can hear, inside his head, the same muck sputtering. Mercy for you, deserter. On the condition that. The army offers you. Amnesty for you.

Your locked eyes pay no attention to the jostling crowd, they torment and measure each other up. Now you are contemplating each other like two lovers after a long separation, withholding complicity that can't quite be revived. The haggard faces croak and rasp around you, you hear bones bending, lungs emptying with a rattle, but nothing breaks this bridge of difficult silence that joins you, and on which neither of you ventures forth.

Machado is the first to open his mouth. He shouts in the patois of the Sixth Battalion, a language you know you are the only ones to. He's giving you information. The soldiers made a truce with the chrysalids. Those bastard soldiers. Several chrysalids have come aboard, as big as orcas, indestructible.

A burst of fire from an automatic weapon rings out in the prow. My mind is covered with a nervous mist. Breathing becomes tenser. Here, aft, we can't see anything. We are left to guess. A second burst, much longer, then the echoes are much more varied. The rattle of cogs, revolver shots. Something explodes, a grenade. Soldiers' shoes run across a metallic surface. The clamor of the crowd increases, decreases, accompanied by a clanking of chains. The soldiers leave the ship. Then the noise of a motor grows more distant across the sea.

A strong waft of fuel fumes suddenly invades the universe.

Machado begins to speak again. Those sons of bitches sold the ship out to the chrysalids. They dropped a motor dinghy into the water. The chrysalids have already barricaded the second bridge. They are dumping barrels of gas on the stairs.

You glance at the lifeboat.

Yes, agrees Machado, it's our only chance to.

Machado comes toward you. Behind him, on a windsock, you notice a poster that hasn't yet had time to yellow with age. You identify the characters one by one and translate them.

Idea of horizontality, mountains.

Circle. Circling. Fortified city.
Three boats. Fire. Deep ocean.

FOR ONE BESEIGED CITADEL ON THE HIGH PLATEAU, THREE CARGO SHIPS AFLAME ON THE OPEN SEA!

VIII

It's for you that. Without you I couldn't.

She's not listening when you talk to her, little brother. You sit side by side on the stony beach. You show Gloria the moon rising above the waves. The horizon glistens. Gloria has always had mysterious distractions, attitudes of refusal, as if locked in a kind of autism. In the shadows, she plays with a fistful of sand. She doesn't look at the moon. She doesn't answer you.

She exists, she doesn't exist. And it's for her, only for her.

IX

But within earshot no beloved appears, little brother. Only Machado is there, parting the magma of piled-up derelicts, and he gets close to you, indicating the two points where your fate has crystallized: on the forward bridge, sixty meters away, the rumbling smoke, outlined by sparks and ribbons of flame, and to the south, an indistinct scar of mercury, showing gray against the sea and signaling the direction of the islands.

And then, you are soldiers.

You have to get hold of the dinghy. Become masters of the dinghy before. Already a man is trying to climb up the davit you're looking at. A madman grabs onto him, cursing. They grapple with each other and, almost immediately, together they fall into the sea. Their example sets off a panicked scramble. A heap of bodies stretches out toward the flying buttresses. Machado calls to you over the chaos.

Veterans!

And already, little brother, with no trouble, without a speck of hesitation, you bray in unison, like during an attack or the sack of a village. You weave the wildness of your cry into his.

Veterans of the Sixth Battalion!

VETERANS OF THE SIXTH BATTALION, REGROUP!

Machado reaches the right-hand davit. As it is keeping you from attaining your goal, the crowd is your enemy. Everything that gets in your way or comes in front of you, you annihilate. You are acting like professionals, with dirty, lightning-fast tactics, surrounded on all sides by the pitiful charades opposing you. Blows don't have time to hurt you. Your hands have forgotten the fever that weakened them that night, that morning. You don't give anyone the chance to take control of your destiny. You break apart mouths, cartilage, you smash collarbones. Machado has acquired a winch handle. You see him spinning in a reddish mist. The people clinging to the davits let them go. The two of you, you do again the dance of death for which you were trained and which is the only reason for your time here among animals and men.

The operation has opened up a provisionally safe space. You can scale the flying buttresses and balance above the sea without risking being hooked or grasped by any nuisances. You leave the support of the rail where you still had one foot and find your balance on the lifeboat, and, while you rip off the tarp to throw it down below, you feel a terrible pain in your side. The exaltation procured by your victory lasts a brief instant, then disappears.

You are crouched in the bottom of the lifeboat, sticky with blood, next to Machado who is shaking the upper pulley of a block and tackle and swearing, because the mechanism is blocked by a security lock located at the base of the davit. You need someone on the bridge to unscrew two wingnuts. You are dangling over the water, separated from the multitude by a laughable gap. The space you made for yourselves has been won back by hysterical shapes. The confusion is too great for you to go back down to undo the wingnuts yourselves.

Mutilated by your presence, the hope of getting into the lifeboat doesn't excite anyone anymore. A man throws a leg over the railing and begins to climb down the ladder. Others follow suit. A fight breaks out. Everyone wants to get onto the rungs before the fire gets here. Exhausted, your teeth chattering, you follow the brawls evolution. Clumsy people are falling from the full height of the ship and crashing into the waves. They try to swim for a moment in the remains of the wake, then sink like stones.

On the cargo ship, the fire rages. The front half of the boat crumbles under a gigantic, oily cloud, continuously shaking and writhing. From the air vents spurt larger and larger flames. The smoke reeks. Eyes water. Heat crackles. It's getting closer.

Machado is yelling instructions in a hoarse but implacable voice. He explains that the lifeboat has to be lowered before loading passengers. He promises passage for everyone. He isn't brandishing the winch handle, it's down against his leg. He has a knee on the floor of the dinghy and he is lecturing the crowd intelligently, mixing the dialects of the Eastern Front with those of the Southeastern. He doesn't threaten. He asks for someone to unscrew the nut on each of the buttresses and he swears that those who do that will be immediately lifted into the lifeboat.

No one seems to understand his speech.

So you yell yourself hoarse in turn, little brother, putting your translation skills to use. You repeat what Machado said, you repeat it several times, varying your intonation. You gesticulate and gesticulate, little brother, exasperated by the ill will of the miserable beings who, on the bridge, could unblock the descent mechanism.

But who don't unblock it.

MONOLOGUE

The wind threw pieces of night forcefully against the door. The lightbulb swung back and forth. Breughel had blotted a few drops of blood beading on his scratches. He had sat back down on the chair. Instead of acting, I was wasting my energy flipping through the accounts of dreams and reasoning over inconsistent elements, over the wrapper for pastries bought in Taipa, over the New Century Hotel in Taipa, without building anything coherent, and I watched this man's movements, with the idea that he was maybe playing some game whose guiding principles I couldn't quite make out, or maybe, on the contrary, he had given up fighting me and was just telling me the truth, no longer giving any value to existence or to lies, seeking annihilation and considering that I was the ideal instrument for that annihilation. He had gathered up the photographs of Gloria and had put them back in the envelope then in the shoebox he had taken them out of some time before. Around us floated the smells of sesame oil and butane gas, then a buffet of wind scattered the contents of a trashcan the length of the alley. The stench flooded into the room. I was suffocating, I continued to be stifled beneath the lamp that was fighting off the shadows with execrable cowardice. Because of the hour, or maybe because the dip in the atmospheric pressure disrupted their self-preservation instinct, the cockroaches strutted between the cardboard boxes, eschewing the dark corners. I saw them move with satisfaction around the depths of things, knowing neither the feeling of failure nor fear of the future. At the end of their path they always found some motive for happy stillness, either a bit of food or a bit of death. I began to envy the cockroaches. My stomach was empty. The fatigue of the trip had lessened at the end of the morning, but now it spread through my body and laid my spirits low. Breughel didn't seem overly affected by the savagery of our last exchange. He went to urinate, then returned. He was a somber being. He was very different from the portraits the Party had collected in the file devoted to him. The ebbing of the tide of all these years had scraped away the layer of patient courtesy behind which he had hidden his face in Europe. Aging had eroded and hardened his physiognomy, deepening his eye sockets and bringing them closer together and giving him, when it came down to it, a slightly idiotic look, a certainly strong-willed but innocent face, with no subtlety, which did not coincide with his psychology as the Party had formerly described it by observing his real personality and scratching the surface of his books. The Party had taken an interest in him, and the reason wasn't idiocy or innocence. I now had under my lamp a sullen intellectual, an entrenched outcast, disguised as a bitter dying man, and all of a sudden I discovered that under the conditions of exile, he must have evolved interiorly to become like his characters. I had unfortunately not had the time nor the energy to read his novels before coming. Breughel coughed. He was waiting. He had already asked me twice if I was going to execute him before dawn. I didn't answer. My brain was running in low gear, without producing any conclusions. The bulb swung with each breath of wind. I would have liked to sit down and eat some kind of meal, then go collapse on clean sheets in a room with air conditioning at the Hotel Peninsula or elsewhere. An anemic thought was fluttering inside my skull. In preparation for my arrival, Breughel had covered hundreds of pages, more, even, perhaps weighing each word with the hope of watching me detour from sentence to sentence until total fusion with the darkness. Now I had shunned incursions in this territory which I felt would have been unfavorable for me. I had read a little, or skimmed without letting myself get carried away. If a plan had been laid out by Breughel on this basis, from these texts I was supposed to read, this plan had failed. Breughel had swallowed his disappointment like he had swallowed my slaps. He was ruminating, breathing morosely, doubtlessly regretting that fate had sent him a killer impervious to his prose, indifferent to literature, to writing, but he didn't moan, and, if he did moan, it wasn't like someone crushed by defeat. Sweat ran down his eyelids. We didn't exchange glances. Outside, the wind kept whistling with no respite. In spite of the walls, we could feel it on the skin of our cheeks, in our hair, around our ankles. The bulb at the end of its wire vibrated and sometimes swung back and forth. From time to time Breughel watched the filament through his eyelashes. Sometimes he seemed mentally defective, sometimes like a subversive ready to take on the whole world. I have to say here, and I won't repeat it, that I felt sympathy for this man. Before I killed him, I had to understand why he hadn't returned to Europe after Gloria Vancouver's death, and why he kept living in a Chinese shack, with no contact with the Chinese and no attachment to Chinese culture and without joy. I still needed to shed light on that. I was tired. I cleared my throat, then I said My mission was never to suppress you, Breughel! I lied in a low voice, soberly, so that he would believe me. The rustling of the wind in the aeration holes competed with my chains of hypocritical syllables. I added, You know, Breughel, Paradise couldn't care less about you, you've always been a nonentity, and then I said It's Machado and Gloria Vancouver that I have to, then I fell silent. The motor of the refrigerator behind my back began to work and hummed away. The noises of the city were muffled by the asthmatic hooting of the alley. We could make out a police siren on the port, the clacking of a carbine issued from a television set, but almost nothing else. The wind dominated everything. I was gathering up Breughel's sensitive property: his Portuguese passport, his keys, the cash I had found during the afternoon, his ATM card from the Banco Nacional Ultramarino, a checkbook from the Hong Kong & Shanghai Banking Corporation. I shoved all of this into my pockets. Breughel was at my mercy, now without identity and without resources I could leave him for a few hours. Nothing kept him, of course, from barricading himself in his house or melting into Macau, but if, as I was convinced, he wanted to survive, he would try to get his papers back and he would try to see me again. I had to leave him with the impression that he was safe. I patted my chest and side pockets and said in a neutral tone I'll give you back part of this mess, under certain conditions, obviously, then I announced that I was going to go eat something somewhere and go to bed. He mumbled a discontented sentence and I said We haven't sorted everything out, Breughel, you're well aware, and I added I'll be back tomorrow or later tonight, don't get too far away, and, as I weighed in my hand the pistol already wrapped in a sheet of the *South China Morning Post*, knowing that I was going to throw it in the nearest bin so it could go join the scrapings of sticky rice, carp scales, and vegetables, he confirmed to me that many little restaurants were open all night near the floating casino and in the whole neighborhood of the Inner Harbour, under the arcades or elsewhere. Then we exchanged a few opinions about Cantonese cooking. Then I advised him not to leave his den and to sleep as best as he could while waiting for morning and my arrival. The lightbulb was swinging again. Something sizzled in the refrigerator's outlet. Breughel complained about not having the key. He grumbled about criminality and the triads, talking about thieves and men ruined at baccarat who prowled in the old port's alleys, ready to use their knives to make good their losses. Suddenly he was fearing for his life and I said It's a risk you'll have to run, Breughel, nothing to be done. Then I left.

FICTION

I

To rejoin Tarrafeiro Street, Kotter staggered in the direction of the lights shining at the end of the alley. His soles slid over vegetable peels, by pure chance avoiding a rat and a puddle. The distance wasn't more than twenty-five meters. A piece of newspaper grazed his left ear. The paper wasn't more disgusting than anything else. It fluttered with a wicked energy against a shop front and disappeared.

Breughel's door let out a creak and went to slam against the wall. The wind must have rushed into the room. You could hear Breughel moving about while the door creaked again and slammed against the wall again. The killer turned around. Barely yellower than the darkness, the bulb's rays died on the threshold of the shack. Remains of manuscript flew above the shadows. Breughel had pushed back a chair and rushed to the opening, but he wasn't yet visible.

After all those hours of inquisition behind closed doors, the exterior air seemed less suffocating, less sticky, and despite the smell of garbage, the warmth had something reinvigorating and even agreeable. The wind was blowing hard, carrying with it a hail of unsanitary crumbs and forcing everyone to walk hunched over, but for the moment the real tropical fury was making us wait. The reality hardly corresponded to what we had imagined when we heard the shattering howls of the shadows.

Breughel got control of the slab of iron protecting his lair from typhoons and bankrupt gamblers and, unmoving, he began to follow Kotter with his eyes. The killer reached Tarrafeiro Street, and, without a backward glance, he disappeared.

He passed the concrete angle that marked the end of the alley, then slid the pistol into one of the trash cans gaping on the sidewalk. Almost immediately he found himself in front of a small restaurant.

The dining room looked like a garage. The walls were empty. Sprinkled with the pale lacquer of neon lights. In a high up alcove a red lamp illuminated a statuette and some incense sticks. The day's menu was taped to a window covered with steam. Kotter stood pensively in front of the esoteric scrawling. He looked at what was on offer in the glass display: Chinese cabbage, a fish head stuck on a hook, kidneys of mediocre mammals.

You could see three Formica tables. On each table were scraps of chicken and a few noodles.

Kotter sat there, avoiding putting his elbows on the bones, in a corner that would allow him to watch the outlet of the alley. He wanted to see if Breughel left his black hole.

A fat man in shorts and a tank top put his sandals on and came to give a swipe with a dishcloth to the table in front of Kotter. He pronounced aggressively a sentence with some relation to the meal, or maybe to the late hour, or to Kotter. The killer got up, pointed to a bowl containing a pile of noodles, then he pointed to a plate where croquettes were stacked in a pyramid, and finally he ran his hand over a shelf and pointed to a can of beer. The man let out another salvo of sounds that displeased Kotter, and then he went to find in the fridge twelve ounces of foamy Tsingtao. Kotter had already settled into his place. He continued to spy on Tarrafeiro Street. It was the location that interested him more than the quality of the service.

People came and went under the lighted sign, unconcerned about the hour, attributing no importance to the gusts of wind. Kotter read the calligraphic inscriptions in krypton in mauve, blue, yellow lamps, then he looked at the invisible faces of passersby.

> Companhia de propaganda TONG NGAI.
> Electricos U CHAN.
> Merceria HAU KEI
> VONG CHI KEI, Estabelecimento de comidas.
> Dentista LO YAT LEUNG.

He seemed captivated by the luminescent combination of Cantonese and Portuguese sounds, and you could see him admiring unrequitedly the severe beauty of passersby but, beneath the surface, his brain was working on the intuitions that, during the evening, had visited it like ghosts, without ever being able to speak to him clearly, not in their embryonic phase.

During his duel with Breughel, Kotter's brain had disappointed him, to say the least. Numbed by the heat and jet lag, it had only seemed capable of initiatives of procrastination. And here it came back to life. Unexpectedly, and while Kotter thought he was in the process of spelling out *CHANG SIO WENG*, Mestre de medicina chinesa, it was formulating a series of very simple hypotheses that finally gave coherence to Breughel's behavior.

Breughel had stayed in Macau, in this world that constantly reminded him of his status as a foreigner, not because he felt at home in the foreign atmosphere, but because an essential element kept him from. And his interest in Guangdong opera wasn't enough to justify the length of his stay, no more so than the depression following his supposed abandonment of Gloria Vancouver's corpse in the Seoul morgue.

Something was keeping him in Macau.

Someone. A woman. A woman who never came to see him, but whom he continued to. His famously psychotic lover. Still alive, very certainly. A memory doesn't enchant a place like that.

And Taipa. This guy visited Taipa often. An island with no particular charm, Breughel's notes and those of the travel guide emphasized that. Empty lots, cemetery, and asylum of. And he. But of course. Gloria Vancouver lived there, she was shut up there, in the madhouse.

And, to trick Paradise's, the Party's envoy, Breughel was putting on his neurasthenic show, with his manuscripts and silences and his nostalgia for death. He had developed a theatrical system. Each detail proved that he was the only survivor of the three renegades, morally beaten down and insignificant. But it was in order to draw attention to himself alone. And so he hoped to suffer the coming punishment alone.

Breughel had his own way of protecting Gloria Vancouver.

Kotter was going to continue his speculations when the proprietor approached him and set a large plate of noodles on the table.

The killer was not a virtuoso at the use of chopsticks, and his fingers got caught up in unnecessary movements. The croquettes that topped the dish had a rubbery texture and tasted like tadpoles. Despite his hunger, Kotter wasn't devouring the food, seeming just to pick at it. The beer, on the other hand, disappeared very quickly. He signaled for another.

In the little dining room open to the wind, two policemen entered and sat down to inhale some soup. The fat man in shorts served them and went back to slump on his chair. He greeted the regular customers with a seemingly less irritable tone than that he had reserved for Kotter.

Above the policemen, a television broadcast pictures of a rocket-launcher fight. It was taking place between heroes inside a hangar or a factory. No one was watching it.

Kotter was keeping a lookout on the street.

An old woman in trousers passed, all in black, topped with a straw hat like in illustrations from mass-market geographical magazines. She was bent in two under a yoke and she shuffled along with her back to the port. There was a spiny mass in her baskets, massive durians, of a somewhat dull green.

At this precise moment, Breughel emerged from the alley. He had put on a windbreaker. He stepped aside to avoid the old woman, and he inhaled the air that whirled in the fruit's passage. Kotter had stiffened. Breughel was progressing slowly. He was walking in the wind that tousled his hair, in the durians' wake, and in order not to fall he clung to memories.

II

Starting in March, April, the durians piled up on the fruit sellers' stalls.

Gloria would ask the seller to cut through the rind with a machete. She liked the pulp with its texture like that of a creamy dessert, like vanilla ice cream melting under a yellow membrane, pale yellow, but which for unadventurous nostrils emits an inelegant smell—repulsive, even—a cocktail of excrement and garlic, with a zest of wet cardboard and a splash of butane.

Gloria held a spoonful of it out to me. An infantile joy sparkled in her eyes. She was suddenly a sly little girl. I knew the matchless flavor of durian flesh, as it matures on your tongue, apple, kiwi, slightly caramelized sugar, tropical flower, but I reluctantly accepted the delicacy she presented to my lips, I feigned disgusted worry, grimacing, seeking to keep in her gaze the light, now so rare, of a little wonder, liking to see laughter blossom in her for a few seconds, in her suffering soul.

III

Breughel passed the greasy spoon and its display and, at first, he noticed only Kotter's two legs and, at eye level, a rectangle of hanging tripe and nests of yellow and light beige noodles, but then he saw Kotter's knees emerging from shorts. On a stool near the sidewalk Kotter had set down his jacket. He could have grabbed it by surprise, complicating the story by involving the forces of order, the law.

Breughel searched the darkness with his gaze, the narrow intersection of which the restaurant occupied one corner, then the thirty meters of street that separated it from the port, from the boulevard, and the lightless mass of debarkation deck number 23, the IAO TAC deck, and having finished this exploration, he came back to the hanging pound of tripe and met Kotter's eyes. He made a resigned, tentative salutation. Desolation stagnated on his whole being.

He went to sit down at the table with Kotter, who was already putting his jacket back on and sweating.

You might have chosen better, he said.

How would I have known? said Kotter.

They stayed silent for half a minute face to face, each on the defensive, eyeing at once the police and the television showing the final conflagration of the hangar with the catastrophic takeoff of a helicopter then its fall into the inferno.

Where were you going? asked Kotter.

Down to the water, said Breughel.

IV

Breughel said Down to the water and, from his body's generally shrunken posture, he suggested that he was going there to throw himself in rather than to watch the waves, but my mind was no longer favorably disposed, my stock of credulity and good will had diminished, and I shrugged my shoulders without answering, satisfying myself with studying Breughel's face, scrutinizing once more his narrowly spaced eye sockets, not lending themselves to the expression of intelligence, and his wrinkles, which in places were much deeper than is usual for a man in his fifties, then his heavy nose, swollen mouth, bruises, hair that sweat and wind had separated into gray feathers and noticing, to conclude, the presence of an open wound near his ear and several scratches on his neck, then I said It's not going well for you, Breughel, I don't believe your little circus act anymore, and I saw that he became suspicious and, after asking me what circus act I was talking about, he leaned forward to hear me more clearly, because the television and the wind covered up the sounds made by my mouth. And anyway I decided not to talk any louder and even on the contrary, to lower the volume of my speech and I said I almost fell for it, Breughel, and I added that he had played his part superbly, with his way of admitting defeat at each intermediate stage of the fight and with his passion for the sordid, for a sordid end, then I whispered But, behind the sadness and fatigue, behind this screen there are the facts, Breughel, the truth about Gloria Vancouver. Breughel was listening to me and, to hide his trembling hands, he soiled them as if by accident in a greasy spot on the table, then he looked for a handkerchief and wiped his hands off. He didn't take his eyes off me. He was avoiding my pupils but he looked at my eyebrows, my lips, my teeth.

So I said I'm not sleepy, then And, besides, I've added an outing to Taipa to my itinerary, and as he blanched immediately, trying nonetheless to pretend that he wasn't turning pale, I said again You'll be my guide, Breughel, you know the way.

He stammered two furred syllables and, at that moment, an aura of hate came over him from head to foot, a piercing vibration whose acidity I could feel on certain sensitive points of my anatomy, like my nail beds, the border of my irises, and then, to keep face, he took on a depressed posture, but he didn't fully achieve the proper slouch. You could see that he couldn't manage to master the animal emotion that seized his insides. His blood was carrying excess adrenaline. His eyelids trembled. I had guessed right. Gloria Vancouver had taken refuge on Taipa. Breughel's body confessed.

After eight seconds he said After all, what could it, then he sighed, and already he was resuming with more success his composure of a disagreeable victim. He grumbled some thought about importance, lack of importance. Around him all malevolent vibrations had dissolved.

Then he said Oh well, OK, Kotter. I'm going to show you what. Since you want.

I nodded my head, not knowing, in fact, what he was agreeing to show me and to avoid revealing the infirmity of my mental constructions, their fragility. It would be better, for me, to speak as little as possible.

Then he said I wonder if, at night, then, as I didn't answer because I was being careful to keep my immobility, to suggest a kind of victorious irony, he said I'm going to buy a lighter to have light in the dark spots, and, as I made no objection, he called to the proprietor dozing on his chair and pronounced two or three sentences in Cantonese, with an ease that astonished me, because I had thought that his knowledge of that language was more approximate. But maybe it is easy to ask for the bill and a lighter in that language.

    I paid. And then, while we were looking for a taxi on the harbor boulevard, he strained his voice to conquer the lugubrious moaning of the wind under the arcades and he said to me Excuse me, Kotter, this afternoon, I had taken you for an imbecile, a dangerous imbecile, but impressionable, manipulable. Then, more quietly, he added While in fact.

V

The driver was a woman of thirty-five or thirty-eight, with sharp cheekbones and small, round ears, without ornament. There was nothing soft and nothing tender about her. You might imagine that her skin had browned over the course of the last period of her life, and that she would continue to dry out and get darker, but without losing a bit of her natural beauty. When she turned back to have us repeat the destination, which she wasn't sure she had heard correctly, as Breughel had placed the tones at random (you can count six or seven tones in the Guangdong language, maybe nine), you could see around her neck a black scarf that made her look like an anarchist. She spoke with a slightly scratchy voice that Breughel loved and which he always gave, in his novels, to his heroines with neither god nor master. Her eyes were hidden behind bluish glasses, glasses like those pirates wear in cities. Breughel abstractly brushed against this unknown comrade, he married her in thought, with a frustrated romanticism that no witness could possibly suspect, then he strung together again the handful of syllables that were at issue. The woman corrected the phonetic mistakes Breughel had made, and then she raised her eyes toward the rear-view mirror, put the car in gear, and started the engine.

Above the taximeter, the clock on board indicated three forty-two A.M.

We'll have to do some walking, said Breughel, I couldn't ask her to stop on the deserted road with the cemetery as her only place to park. Not at this hour, you see.

You're the one who sees, Breughel, said Kotter.

He had held back from showing his astonishment when Breughel had said where they.

The driver took hold of a microphone and spoke for a few seconds by radio with the night taxi dispatcher, maybe to signal her direction, maybe to ask about the typhoon's progress toward the territory, maybe for the simple pleasure of hearing Cantonese unsullied by foreigners. Her fingers stuck out of not-very-clean cotton mitts, unraveled between the index and middle fingers.

It was cool inside the vehicle now driving by the harbor facilities, then going up Almeida Ribeiro Avenue, they started out on the Taipa bridge. The traffic was sparse. In front of the Lisboa Hotel, the flashing lights of a patrol lit up the tangle of bicycle rickshaws. The naked legs of sleeping men stuck out of the cabs.

The driver had inserted a cassette into her stereo. You could easily recognize *The Sobs of San Pak before the Lotus Offering*. San Pak's lamentation was sometimes interrupted by the radio's crackling, when the dispatcher began or finished a conversation with this or that nocturnal vehicle.

The taxi had reached the middle of the bridge.

Kotter fought against sleep. The closed windows and the music tempted him to drop off.

He began to inspect the panorama, the sumptuously illuminated shoreline by the Hotel Lisboa, from the Bank of China skyscraper to the floodlights of the Outer Harbour, and, on the other shore, in Taipa, the more isolated masses indicating the university, the New Century Hotel, the Hyatt, the new apartment complexes. You could also see, in the distances, a few lights shining in the People's Republic.

It's beautiful, Kotter commented.

Yes, said Breughel. San Pak is mourning his love. He is going to die. He is alone.

VI

Kotter yawned. For very short fractions of a second, he dozed off and dreamed. He immediately emerged, but this loss of vigilance didn't. He didn't appreciate it.

Once in Taipa, the car flew down the coast road and passed flashing advertisements for the casino at the Hyatt Hotel, then it turned in front of the New Century Hotel. It took the avenue of which a hundred meters followed the gardens and huts of the shantytown. The shantytown being situated lower than the road, Kotter didn't see anything except maybe the garlands of red lightbulbs leading to the **HONG KEI** restaurant.

Because of who-knows-what holiday or celebration, triangular banners floated over the median, in the middle of the street. Pink, light blue, yellow, black pennants with inscriptions and lacy edges, white when a background was needed for dark writing.

The wind twisted and shook all this frenetically.

You'd think it was a period film, said Kotter. Flags around a Chinese military camp, you think? During the Three Kingdoms, right?

Oh, I don't know about the Three Kingdoms, said Breughel.

After expanses of fallow land and towers under construction, they arrived at the intersection beyond which the old village of Taipa began. The driver slowed down and without taking her eyes off the road, by a movement of her neck, let it be known that she was waiting on instructions from her passengers. Breughel pointed at the entrance to a street, a little building, trash cans. The car went there and stopped.

I told her to leave us here, said Breughel.

You're in charge, Breughel, said Kotter.

I don't have a cent, you took everything off me, said Breughel, pointing to the meter.

Kotter took a bill of fifty patacas out of his pocket and held it out to the woman pirate. She leaned forward to fumble in the box where she kept the change.

Leave a good tip, said Breughel.

How much? asked Kotter.

She should keep the change, said Breughel.

But the trip was only thirty patacas, objected Kotter.

Breughel opened the door and got out. Kotter hurried after him, not without having expressed with his hand his disdain for dollars. The woman didn't thank him, she pushed the automatic closure and the door slammed. Then the car maneuvered and tuned back to the roundabout. Already it was heading toward the banners of the Three Kingdoms.

Twenty patacas for a tip, grumbled Kotter.

And so? said Breughel. It's not going to put the Party out in the street.

The howling of the wind forced the two to strain on their vowels. Other complaints from Kotter were lost. The killer didn't like waste, but less than everything else did he appreciate staying permanently etched in the memory of a woman who drove a taxi with a black scarf around her neck.

Is it far? he finally asked.

No, said Breughel.

Eh! Are we going far? repeated Kotter.

The wind was puffing so hard that Breughel's response had gone unnoticed.

VII

They made their way along the side of the road. They climbed the hill. The grade was steep. Every fifty meters stood a lamppost. On both sides the vegetation was twisting tumultuously. Bushes of scrub, pines, Chinese figs, Mandarin thujas, parasol trees, and worse, privet, cheesewoods, sophora, *kōwhai*, and worse yet. The wind attacked the leaves, the branches, and in spite of the collective gesticulation facing it, tried to mangle anything living and weak. It clawed at everything continuously.

Kotter closed the zipper of his jacket. He had distributed among its many pockets Breughel's papers and money, the junk Smith & Wesson, a notebook where he had read a short while before *Chrysalids of the Ninth Banner*, *Pirates of the Quicksilver Seas*, and other Breughelian ineptitudes.

On the left is the cemetery, said Breughel.

What? yelled Kotter.

There, pointed Breughel.

I don't see anything, said Kotter.

Behind the trees, everywhere, shouted Breughel. Chinese graves. The hill is covered with graves.

Ah, said Kotter.

The squalls threw them from side to side. Sometimes they bumped into each other. They walked like drunks.

As he staggered forward, Kotter wondered. Did Breughel really want to reveal a key element of the Vancouver file to him? What good was it following Breughel into a cemetery? Was this a new strategy to distance him from Gloria Vancouver. And what if, despite his physical disadvantage, Breughel was up to no good?

Right after this, I'll be taking over the operation, warned Kotter.

After what, said Breughel.

They found themselves under a streetlight whose bulb had burned out. The metallic pole sang in the wind. The two men progressed, squinting their eyes in the squall. Knowing that no one could gauge the exact distance between his lashes, Kotter kept his eyelids closed for a few seconds. It was nice to doze against the wind, with no other concern than to keep his balance.

This way, said Breughel.

Kotter interrupted his nap, made the best of it, then stepped over the rail that bordered the curve in the path. Beyond, between the bushes, two cement steps appeared, gray. They were at the entrance to one of the many paths leading to the dead's resting places. Breughel had almost disappeared in the branches of a very nervous Cantonese spirea.

Eucalyptus leaves stabbed Kotter's face. Other leaves, of another species, danced on the horizon, detached from everything.

Hey Breughel, wait, yelled Kotter, don't do any.

What foolishness, protested Breughel.

Kotter started up the steps. Breughel was two or three meters ahead. He caught up with him. They were now shadows in the shadows, on a new fragment of stairs leading to a little terrace. The vegetation hindered the light coming from the road. On our retinas was a constant alternation between diluted inky black and shadow. At the entrance to the esplanade, two pillars held up dwarf lions in blue porcelain. You could see, at the end, the tomb and its grayish curves like those of a sleeping elephant, submerged among the plants. The parasol trees crackled and creaked around them.

Breughel, obviously, knew where he was going. He passed this tomb and jumped down lower, onto a second esplanade, marked out by two tall cement curves, and then he threaded his way between the trunks of pines and began to descend. The slope was rough, sometimes broken up by five or six degrees of stone, sometimes not. The path had little logic and was full of stumbling stones. They passed by holes, walking on the far edge of terraces, and, beyond those, the privet whipped the air and shrieked.

We're almost there, said Breughel.

None too soon, said Kotter. You need the lighter?

Oh, with this wind, refused Breughel.

He was crouched in front of a gravestone, near a tripod of offerings. Pine needles and eucalyptus whirled on the ground without their crackling being distinguishable in the din. Kotter was listening to the bellows announcing the typhoon's arrival, the insane howling of the hill, but he wasn't communing with nature. He danced from one foot to the other. Again he closed his eyes as if he wanted to sleep standing up.

What are you looking for, he asked.

I made a mistake, said Breughel, standing up. It's somewhere else.

Somewhere else? Kotter said indignantly.

I mixed up two paths, said Breughel. It's more to the right, a hundred meters.

I suppose we'll have to climb back up, complained Kotter.

Yes, said Breughel.

He went around the killer and he pointed to a narrow ten degrees leading to a new funerary esplanade with a cement table and benches.

That way, he said.

They started off again in the labyrinth. Kotter now followed close on Breughel's heels with the certainty that he was not trying to fool him. The mistake had restored the confidence between the two being.

Then, who knows why, after having stepped over a dead tree, Kotter was two or three meters in front of Breughel, and, just as he was going to say that he couldn't see anything, he felt around his neck a cutting wire strangling him.

So Breughel.

So Breughel hadn't been beaten or discouraged, and he had set up an ambush without ever letting his impatience show through, hiding his villainy under false resignation, beneath a craven exterior, lulling to sleep one by one the killer's suspicions, leading him to an unlikely place, lurking and waiting for the chance to act. And not hesitating, when the moment came to. He had taken advantage of the darkness to take from his pocket something like a string of a violin or Chinese lute, *jing hu* or *si hu* or *xian xi*, not that it matters, or electric wire, any kind of lasso. He had thrown the murderous slipknot around Kotter's head and was pulling him backwards. And he was pulling with all his strength, obviously, with the evident plan of killing Kotter, getting rid of him and still and still protecting Gloria Vancouver.

Like all his kind, Kotter had the skills of an elite soldier. He had taken the self-defense courses given in Paradise's schools. To each attack corresponded parries, matched with counterattacks during which the assailant was ripped apart or slain. Strangulation made up its own chapter, more nuanced. Everything depended on the adversary's skills, on his. If the opponent showed any hesitation, if their position behind the strangled person lacked foresight, he was lost. Otherwise, no.

Kotter had just exhaled when the loop took him prisoner. The wire stabilized underneath his Adam's apple and penetrated his skin, while Breughel crushed the inside of his knee joint to prevent him from turning around as he fell. Kotter felt his coccyx sit violently down onto the gravel and leaves. He had vainly tried to slide a hand under the wire. His situation didn't favor any movement of the torso or limbs. Behind him, well placed, master of the technique, Breughel said nothing and pulled. About two thirds of a second had passed since the beginning of the ambush.

Then a whole second passed, then a handful more. The wind swept the area.

Kotter was in pain.

He fought breathlessly.

Then, his consciousness and.

His consciousness and memory derailed.

He was losing his identity. He was dreaming that he had come very far to die, at 22°16′ of latitude and 113°35′ of longitude east. He had stopped time. He had been shut up for years in a fetid shadow. He no longer knew who he. Behind the door of a shack he was making up stories like Breughel did, he was becoming one of Breughel's characters, and dedicating his life to nothing and to Gloria Vancouver, he was becoming Breughel.

He still hadn't caught his breath.

Now, he was Breughel.

MONOLOGUE

I got up.

I was covered with dead leaves and dirt. I brushed off my jacket. The tempest surrounded me. The trees tried to rip my face open. The wind sent me up against a moaning trunk. A burning sensation ran down my back, around my neck, between my shoulders. The cartilage of my fingers hurt.

I was panting.

The rain began to splash down and, with no transition, the universe liquified. The heavy oblique draperies beat down on Taipa, on the muddy construction sites and on the cemeteries. The wind had strengthened. A branch broke above my head and bounced off the funerary esplanade, next to the spot where I was trying with great effort to maintain my balance. The eucalyptus whipped each other and bent over. The heat was still exhausting. It had lowered by a degree but not more. A torrent began to pour down the steep path I would have to climb if I wanted to get back to the road. Little frothy waves splashed from step to step. The darkness grew deeper. My heart thumped. I couldn't calm down. None of my muscles could relax. Around me, the world broke apart and crashed.

I began thinking of Gloria Vancouver. She had woken up and couldn't go back to sleep. The wing of the hospital where she was lodged seemed to be hermetically defended from the typhoon's assaults, but the windows shook, the doors vibrated in their grooves.

The doors are vibrating in their grooves.

The window is shaking.

Gloria's eyes are wide open onto the noisy heat. She has given up on sleep. She is breathing in the smells of mildew and the emanations from the lower floors, the sticky rice soup and schizophrenics' sweat. She sits up in the middle of the bed. She's listening to the typhoon take hold of the night.

A gecko has found shelter in her room. It flattens its ten centimeters on the silent motor of the air conditioner. The nightlights in the hallway and the lights from the courtyard help to make out its humble form. To save energy and for security reasons, electricity is cut to the patients at night. Gloria flips the switch that controls the ceiling light, then murmurs a protest against the nuns' stinginess. Now she opens a drawer and feels around. She picks up a flashlight Breughel gave her. She lights it.

She has left her bed.

She stands under the gecko. She contemplates its slenderness for a long time, she admires the two beads of jet it has for eyes, then she turns off the flashlight. She doesn't like to see her reflection in the windowpane, her face lit from below like in a horror movie. She draws closer to the window. She looks at the courtyard. The trees are contorted. The ground has disappeared. Beyond the water and leaves, the **FONG KUOK CHAK** wing looks like a waterfall. On the left, in a gap in the branches you can see the old folks' building. The shantytown is invisible. In the distance, on the construction sites, the lights of the cranes pierce the black space. In case of a storm, the booms aren't locked in place, they point in the direction the wind is blowing, and, in the illumination of their lights, the flood undulates horizontally.

The flood is undulating, says Gloria.

Horizontally, she continues in a murmur.

She's talking to the lizard frozen above her head. She watches its reaction, simplifying her speech so it can understand. She speaks in a melodious mix of Portuguese, English, and Chinese. None of these languages is her native language. Like in Breughel's books where the characters, at one point or another of their catastrophe, end up lecturing insignificant and obscure animals, Gloria offers her voice to the lizard, a few remarks on the overflowing of nonlight, or on the thickness of the layer of water that.

At any rate, the gecko doesn't show any sign of intelligence, and, after a minute, she formulates a last whisper in Cantonese, then falls silent.

Her knowledge of the Guangdong language has been acquired in dormitories, at the cafeteria, under the big trees of the courtyard. She's had for teachers old incontinent prostitutes, madwomen, old beggars. Each one had a name and a story, a personal tragedy that she relives day after day or has sealed off, once and for all, behind her empty gaze.

Gloria herself doesn't confide much in the other patients. She is interned with a Portuguese identity and her medical file contains the explanation furnished by Breughel, fables that were archived then abandoned. No doctor had had the chance to be surprised by the atypical oddities of her case. There is no psychiatric care in the institution. They had taken Gloria in out of charity and because they had the assurance that fees for her stay would be paid regularly. The nuns don't make any fuss about keeping her.

Her condition is stable. She couldn't live in the outside world. She dedicates her waking hours to meditation, but she also passes through phases of verbal violence. When she is hallucinating, when she is telling about her dreams, the civil war on earth or elsewhere, when she screams at the chrysalids not to take vengeance, so that the boats coming to the islands aren't burned on the high seas, no one can echo her anxiety, reassure her or contradict her. No one is near her who might know Paradise's jargon. Her ravings are like the spectral sob of a dog or a cat or a little girl tortured by humans. You don't know what species her plaintive cry belongs to. The nuns guess that something unbearable is happening. They enter the room, they take bodily hold of Gloria. Neither harshness nor gentleness calms her down. On the floor above, in sympathy, the patients sob.

Gloria listens. A woman on the ground floor is no longer accepting the present as it is. She is calling for help. Despite the moaning of the shadows, her cries can be heard.

At the same time, in the courtyard, a shape is zigzagging from one shadow to the next and, clings to a fig tree trunk in front of the **FONG KUOK CHAK** wing. The night watchman maybe.

But no. The watchman wouldn't go out like that in the torrential rain and wouldn't move around trying to stay out of the light of the outside lamps, like a thief.

Breughel, then. It's the kind of thing he would do.

Breughel comes to the hospital as much as possible. He keeps Gloria's mental ruin company. An irreversible destruction has happened inside his friend, but nothing has been broken between the two beings. His presentation of his relationship with Gloria had been a lie. Contrary to reality, of the fatigue and hate that had grown between the couple in front of Kotter, not a note was the truth. Their affection had not been corrupted. Tenderness persists. Breughel does not regret meeting Gloria, he doesn't have any qualms about having fled with Gloria far from the certainty and cultures that shaped his first life, there at the other end of the world. He knows that with Gloria and Gloria's madness he has reached a terrible final chapter. But he loves Gloria more than. And he loves the idea that in calling down on himself alone Paradise's brutality, he is making his way without dishonor to his final paragraph. Let's not lose sight of the literary angle from which Breughel has always considered his own existence and that of others, these decades of diluted and ruminated reality called existence.

Breughel meets Gloria during visiting hours, he distracts her, he tells her about his comings and goings in the alleys of the Inner Harbour, at the markets. He describes the crowds of strangers, here a beggar with deformed feet, martyred, there the infinitely many pretty girls with their nongazes and their noisy eructations. He takes her step by step with him on the walks he has taken through the cemeteries of Macau and Taipa, he tells her about the graves, the offerings, he invents opera performances, *Meeting at the Capital* in the open air in front of the Tou Tei temple, *The Chiu Family's Orphan* under a roof by the Lin Kai temple, under bamboo structures, in the torrid steam, and the traffic noises, with the hubbub of the audience that never lessens. He tells her the plots of operas, movies, and novels. He creates the scenes for her. From the interior night common to the two of them, he has brought forth a detective whose mission is to execute them. He names him Kotter. Sometimes John Kotter, sometimes Dimitri. Always Kotter.

In general, Gloria stays taciturn, on the edge of her bed or under the trees, while Breughel lists images, but sometimes she happens to speak. She confides a scrap of a dream in Breughel, then is quiet. She doesn't mention Paradise, nor the special section she worked for called Grandmother. She never alludes to her activities as Grandmother's agent. Even in the depths of mental confusion, Grandmother's agents maintain their obsession with secrets and camouflage, and it would require a good deal more than a break in their personality to shatter their prudence. Between Grandmother and her agents, what is organic can break or betray, but not ideological ties. Faithful to Paradise, they all remain in their hearts.

Faithful to Paradise Gloria remains in her heart. Never will she repent, never will she consort with the enemy.

Breughel supports her in this resolution.

And so a few hours pass. Then Breughel has to leave the hospital.

He roams around the area. Soaked with sweat, he walks around the old folks' home, then walks by the madhouse again, with its loudspeakers from which the nuns give instructions to the community, then, when dusk falls, he listens to the anxious groans, the inarticulate cries that multiply in the **LEUNG CHEUNG** wing, in **FONG KUOK CHAK**, in **SIU WA NGAI** number two.

He never has the strength to leave for Macau. He dawdles. The mosquitoes devour him. He waits for night to fall. Sometimes he goes into the shantytown. He walks on the planks that separate the ditches. Sometimes he orders some grilled meat at the restaurant there. When he has eaten, he leans against a pillar under the garland of red lightbulbs. He raises his head, looks at the dense volume of the fencerow. On the right, the hedges are eaten up by parasitic plants. You can't see much of the buildings where the mad are trying to resist life and death at the same time. And that's when an inhabitant of the shantytown walks across the grass of the leant-to, next to him, next to the bottles of gas. She appears, lit by the red rays of the sign and the lamps. She's carrying a basket of laundry and, on her hip, a sleeping baby. You can see her flawless features, her round face, her very slender mouth, made inflexible by a hard life. You would like to spend a little time with her, a few hundredths of a unit of time, to wander until you get to her mother's or young woman's eyes.

You would like, thinks Gloria, to share a little of the time of her inflexible eyes. A few hundredths of her round sleeping face. To wander until.

Her daydream suddenly scatters. Something unknown has happened outside her field of consciousness, that she has registered and is now troubling her.

She moves. Condensation dampens her forehead. She glances at the gecko. It begins a movement toward the alcove where the air conditioner is embedded and, again, it freezes. The spot where it would have liked to hide is too wet. The rain strafes the fan, the lid of the apparatus.

The walls are vibrating.

You can feel the wind inside the bedroom. A misty draft passes through the bricks. It moistens Gloria's cheeks. A stream of water trembles the length of the window. It branches out, then reaches the ground. The lamps of the courtyard, often hidden by branches, don't provide enough light to.

Gloria puts her left hand on the wall, on the nightstand, on the radio whose batteries have died and which broadcasts neither meteorological information nor excerpts of *Rain on the Leaves of the Pagoda Trees*. The plaster is sticky. The radio is sticky.

The radio was also sticky. Everything was warm to the touch.

Gloria put her face up to the glass. She was dressed in a very light, very white nightgown.

That allowed me to see her.

I leaned against one of the trees. It was as if I was drunk from the chaos and the blows, immobile. I peered at the windows. The wings were dismally identical. My eye was attracted to this scarcely discernable presence behind the ferocious striations and froth, and then I recognized her. I put a name to the apparition. I called softly Gloria, Gloria Vancouver. And I smiled.

I was lucky. I could have very well languished there, wrapped up in the cataclysm, under the lifeless windows, with nothing to reward my patience.

I was one with the shadow. The bark was smooth. I was one with the assaults of the wind. I hung onto the barbarity of the wind without establishing a border between it and the depths of my flesh. The rain whistled along with the speed of a saber blow. Tons of black transparency were flying at low altitude and slamming into me, they buried me, and, as soon as I regained my senses, they assaulted me again. I was one with the rushing water. I had in me these noises of rage and these abysses. The water gurgled around my ankles. The branches thrashed until they nearly broke. The sapwood tree shook beneath my fingernails. I stared one by one at the submerged façades, lit by lamps. On the old folks' wing, a piece of corrugated metal had come loose from the roof and was crawling away with long scrapings and bellows, in the hope of finally reaching the abyss.

Gloria is breathing with irregular gasps.

She is more nervous than she was a short while ago.

She looks at the cement benches, the shining surfaces, the trees doing everything they can not to perish. The man has changed his shelter. He is pressed against another fig tree. He's closer. He's no longer moving. His silhouette is a vegetal outgrowth. He is avoiding the light. His jacket looks like Breughel's windbreaker.

In the dormitory on the floor below, the hysterical fit is not getting calmer. Someone begins to curse the typhoon. Other patients follow the example and hurl strident prayers against the din. It seems like a general melee has broken out. The LEUNG CHEUNG wing is filled with cries. Gloria, in turn, shouts a handful of slogans that. Naked chrysalids, soldiers immobile under the ashes. In vain vocal cords vibrate. In vain they beg. The manifestations of irrational distress inspire no scruples in the hurricanes. As for the nuns, they're sleeping in SIU WAI NGAI number two. They never bother to interrupt the little nocturnal insurrections. They are used to. They've decided not to be moved anymore. They wait for the morning.

The windows are bowed in beneath the force of the wind, the walls grunt. In the new building, you can hear the windows explode pane by pane.

Gloria has stopped yelling. She cleans off the mist she's exhaled, which blocks her view of the courtyard. She resumes her lookout.

The typhoon's power increases yet again.

The rain is so dense that the cranes on the construction sites are no longer visible.

Over by the old folks' wing an uprooted tree swims against the current. It is drowning. It is seeking a resting place. It jumps. The branches slap the waves. You fight like that when you know you're going.

The level eight signal must have been raised. The Taipa bridge must have. Fearing the prohibition of traffic between Macau and the islands, Breughel must have.

It's he who.

The man's silhouette. The courtyard. Disappeared. Is a disaster scene.

Gloria is no longer looking at anything. Eyes empty, she sits down across from the window. She's breathing. Her bare feet are on the warm tiles. She is sitting on the edge of her bed. She is listening to what comes and goes. She hears steps in the corridor. She's thinking of Breughel who. With affection, she's thinking of Breughel. The door opens. She doesn't turn around. She knows that Breughel. She's thinking of Breughel. She's thinking about the islands. She shakes her hair very gently. She pushes it back very gently. She uncovers her neck, her shoulder, imperceptibly, so that Breughel can.

ANTOINE VOLODINE is an author and translator who has to date published forty-eight novels in French under various names, including *Solo Viola* (2021) and *Mevlido's Dreams* (2024), both published by Minnesota. He has won many literary awards, including the prestigious Medici Prize for 2014's *Terminus radieux*.

GINA STAMM is associate professor of French at The University of Alabama in Tuscaloosa. They are translator of *Mevlido's Dreams* (Minnesota, 2024).